A neon sign in the parking lot next door kept blinking on and off, illuminating the room with bluish light every other second. The bathroom door was slightly ajar and a sliver of light lay across the ragged carpet.

She heard the toilet running, and forced herself to push the door gently. It creaked and opened wider by itself in the slight draft flowing through the hall.

A single light bulb lit the small room beyond. The woman was sprawled on the floor with her head against the toilet bowl and her mournful eyes staring like two brown marbles.

Her throat was cut from ear to ear.

D1602996

LUCILLE
FLETCHER

AVON BOOKS ◆ NEW YORK

AVON BOOKS
A division of
The Hearst Corporation
105 Madison Avenue
New York, New York 10016

First Avon Books Printing: April 1990

AVON TRADEMARK REG. U.S. PAT. OFF. AND IN OTHER COUNTRIES, MARCA
REGISTRADA, HECHO EN U.S.A.

Printed in the U.S.A.

RA   10   9   8   7   6   5   4   3   2   1

To my daughters,
Taffy and Wendy,
and my grandsons,
Douglass and James

PROLOGUE

On a beautiful Sunday morning in October 1969, Robin Cho-doff, aged eight, and her four-year-old sister, Marya, went for a walk with their mother in Central Park.

It had rained the night before and the paths were littered with wet autumn leaves. Marya was wearing new patent-leather shoes, which kept slipping on the pavement, so her mother held her hand and told Robin to do the same. With the Plaza Hotel retreating behind them, they walked slowly down the winding path leading from the park entrance to the zoo.

Robin could hear ducks quacking in the sunny pond below, and looked across the grass for her favorite white duck. But mostly she watched her mother's face and wondered what she was thinking. So far she hadn't said a word about their father going away with all his suitcases the night before.

Marya had been asleep but Robin was still awake when he peeked into their room and came tiptoeing up to her bed. His gray eyes were bright as he bent down and kissed her. "Be a good girl, honey," he whispered huskily, "and from time to time think of your old father, OK?" Then he was gone, a stocky bearded figure with shaggy black hair sneaking out into the hall, where his suitcases were standing.

"Daddy!" she called, but he picked up the suitcases and a second or two later she heard the apartment door slam.

Her mother's fingers were cold but Marya's small hand was warm, and she kept tugging against Robin's fingers as though she wanted to be free to run. Her brown eyes danced above her pink dress and navy-blue blazer and her long brown wavy hair floated around her shoulders, glittering in the sun.

Marya was a "beauty." Everybody said so. People noticed her wherever she went and said she looked like a doll or a Poly-nesian maiden, or the image of her mother. No one complimented Robin. At eight she was in the gawky stage and missing a couple of teeth. Marya commanded all the attention, except for their mother, who was always being asked, "Say, aren't you the girl in *All Our Tomorrows* . . . the one who plays Francesca?"

"No, I'm sorry," her mother would usually say with a shy smile. "I wish I *were* Francesca, but I'm just a housewife and mother."

She was lying, for of course she was Francesca and had been on *All Our Tomorrows* for three years. She was famous, with her picture splashed on magazine covers at supermarkets, and even on movie-theater posters.

She was going to make another movie before Christmas, and that was why Daddy had left. They had been fighting ever since the contract had been signed.

Robin had heard some of the arguments through the walls of her room, which was next door to theirs. "I don't see why you can't tell those jerks to go to hell instead of working during the holidays. If you're going to be an artist, then *act* like one, for God's sake," he had said.

And she had answered, "It's not a matter of artistry, Leo. I promised to do it, and the money *is* important."

"You mean *I* don't bring in enough, is that what you're saying?" Up and down went the angry voices, while Robin lay listening anxiously in the darkness.

She didn't know whose side she was on. She thought her mother, with her violet eyes and masses of dark hair, was gorgeous and deserved all the praise in the world. But she also loved her father, whom she greatly resembled, and felt that if she'd been his wife, she'd never go near Hollywood.

Maybe the trouble was that her father was home a lot, whereas her mother was out all the time, leaving him to baby-sit. Her father was a symphony conductor, but he didn't get many jobs, so he usually spent the day slopping around in his pajamas and bedroom slippers, with his spiky black hair sticking up from his head, playing the Steinway so loudly the neighbors complained. Or else he would stand in his bathrobe in front of the bathroom-door mirror, waving his baton while the stereo played Prokofiev's "Piano Concerto" or the "Leningrad Symphony" by Dimitri Shostakovich until again the phone rang and Mrs. Finch on the floor below started yelling.

But now he had gone away with his baton and his music scores and even his full-dress suit. When Robin looked in his closet, it was gone. Walking along beside her mother, she felt as though her heart would break. Who cared about the seals and the monkeys when he wouldn't be there when they got back to the apartment? And where was he? He was so sad in his crumpled pajamas and bedroom slippers. On this Sunday morning she pictured him all alone sitting on a subway with his suitcases, or smoking cigarettes and pulling at his hair in some dark little hotel room.

"Oh, excuse me, ma'am, but aren't you Francesca?"

Two fat women were blocking their path to the zoo. One was seated in a wheelchair with a brown velvet tam on her enormous balloonlike head. The other one, the one who had spoken, was smiling at her mother with a mouth in which there were only a few teeth.

"My daughter and I—we're just crazy about your show. She's not herself, you see, but she just smiles and smiles whenever you come on the screen. Could you sign something for my poor darling, please?"

After a quick look at the woman in the wheelchair, Robin's mother said yes, of course, and began fumbling in her pocketbook.

But she couldn't find a pencil or a decent piece of paper.

Meanwhile, the mother of the woman in the tam kept talking about the show and Francesca and her long-term lover, Dr. Hays Stanfield, and was Francesca really going to ditch him and move in with Gary Moffatt, even though he was a hopeless alcoholic? And Robin's mother kept looking through her purse and smiling, and trying to answer the woman's questions. She was really very kind and polite.

"I wouldn't bother you so much, but it means so much to my Florence. She'll sleep with it under her pillow."

Robin and Marya grew more and more restless.

"Could we just walk to the steps, Mommy?" Robin asked. "I'll look after her."

For a second her mother hesitated. Then she made the decision she would regret for the rest of her life.

"All right, kiddies, but don't go any farther," she said. "Stay where I can see you." As the children started off, she called, "And don't let go of her hand, Robin."

They walked slowly, hand in hand, down the winding path.

They passed a soldier with one leg, leaning against a tree with one of his trouser legs folded and fastened to his shirt with a huge safety pin. They passed a tall man with blond bangs, holding a big brown poodle on a leash. Marya wanted to pat the dog, but the man glared at her and tugged the poodle back, so they walked on, with Robin still holding tight to her sister's moist hand. Next came two old men playing checkers on a bench, and just before they reached the steps leading down to the zoo, they came upon an old lady dressed in black with a shopping bag at her feet.

As they came toward her she spied Marya and sat up straighter on the bench. She was scary-looking, with a long black veil falling on either side of her straggly gray hair. Marya was fascinated. She loved witches and spooks.

Pink-cheeked and round-eyed, she stood on the path staring.

"Allo . . ." Rising from her bench like a snake from its hole, the old lady grinned and croaked in a foreign accent, "Come 'ere, my leetle beauty. Come 'ere and let me see you."

Marya gave a frightened gasp, and tugging her hand loose from Robin's, tried to hide behind Robin's skirt. As the old woman advanced toward her, cackling endearments and baring yellow teeth, Marya shrieked and fled toward the shallow steps, slipping and sliding in her new shoes on the fallen leaves, then disappearing among the crowds surging up from the zoo.

"Marya . . . !"

Robin raced after her.

The park had never seemed so crowded. Hordes of people filled the sunny zoo plaza. In the shadow of the red-brick, castlelike building there were balloon men, ice cream vendors, pinwheel sellers, mothers with baby carriages, and children of all ages running about.

"Marya! Marya!"

Robin darted back and forth, pausing to sweep the plaza with her eyes. After all, Marya was just a baby. Once she found herself alone, she would start looking for Robin or her mother.

"Marya . . . !"

There was no sign of her.

Robin's heart began to flutter.

Maybe Marya was hiding on purpose. She loved games and teasing people. She would wriggle under a bed or hide in a closet and then jump out with a delighted shriek. She was a born actress like her mother and already doing imitations of her favorite toy animals, Goldie the lion cub and Zumgolly the chimp.

"Marya . . . !"

With a sick feeling in her stomach, Robin raced over to the seal pool. It glittered green in the sun. She could hear the seals barking. "Marya . . . where are you, Marya? Come on, Marya. That's mean!" Around the seal pool was a wall of bodies. She wormed her way in between legs in blue jeans, dresses, and panty hose. "Please let me by, lady. I'm looking for my sister. She has brown hair, in a blue jacket, a pink dress. Will you *please* help me, sir?"

She felt a hand grab her shoulder.

"*Where's Marya?*"

It was her mother, tall and white-faced, teetering on high heels. As Robin tried to explain, her mother wheeled away from her and began to run across the sun-filled plaza. "Marya! Marya!" Her voice grew faint and died away. It was part scream, part sob. Elbowing her way through the tides of moving people, her mother ran up the steps of the terrace restaurant, past the gay umbrellas, and vanished from view.

"Mommy, wait for me . . . !"

But her mother did not return and there was only the plaza with its pushing, shoving crowds. The skyscrapers glared down like giant walls of gleaming rock. And though Robin kept searching, no Marya was in sight—not even in front of the animal cages, where the wolves paced back and forth and the monkeys on their trapezes dribbled banana skins and orange rinds on the wet floor of their cage.

A siren began to wail.

Robin's mother reappeared, followed by a policeman. She was wearing one shoe. Her face was streaked with tears and eye makeup. "She hasn't come back?" she cried out to Robin. "Oh my God, where *is* she? What happened to her? Where did she *go?*"

Grasping Robin's wrist, she jerked her to and fro with a demented light in her eyes. And the hysterical questions, the frenzied behavior, were like knives in the young child's heart. Then, like a rag doll, her mother slid to her knees, and laying her head on Robin's skinny little shoulder, burst into sobs, wracking, shuddering sobs, as Robin began to cry too.

1

ON MANY A SPRING MORNING a slender figure could be seen running against the sun rising above New York's East River.

Dressed in shorts and a white T-shirt, with a bright head-scarf bound around her long straight black hair, Robin Chodoff, now aged twenty-six, ran with the grace of a practiced runner. For an hour or two, with the sun on her face, she could feel one with the other young people of the city. She could believe that life was rich and filled with camaraderie and promise.

She ran early in the morning, when the streets were quiet and empty and the cool light of dawn gilded the bridges and skyscrapers. She loved the fierce green river that hurled itself between its cement banks, fighting its way through the canyons of Manhattan toward the huge black span of the Triboro Bridge and the swirling currents of Hell Gate.

Running along the familiar path had become an antidote to her mother's dying. It helped ease the loss of her beloved father, who had died alone in London the year before with no one except her to attend his funeral, even though he had become a famous conductor, well known for his sensitive interpretations of Delius and other English composers.

In that hour of fresh air, with the wind and sun in her face, she could almost forget the gnawing guilt and shocking pain of that October morning eighteen years before when Marya had disappeared in Central Park, never to be seen again.

Never since that morning had Robin entered Central Park. Although it was rife with runners, she had never even crossed it in a cab, however inconvenient. To her it was a place accursed.

She kept to the East Side of the city and avoided the West. Climbing a flight of steps at East Eight-first Street and East End Avenue, she emerged onto a wide dazzling promenade filled with sunlight and flanked by apartment houses. Across the river lay the long hazy tip of Roosevelt Island, with its cluster of buildings, and ahead lay Wards Island, where pheasants roamed wild amidst weeds and deserted baseball diamonds, and murder victims were occasionally dumped in the dead of the night.

Down the river, a splendid sailboat was sweeping toward her.

She paused to watch it. Laughing people were on board and a young man in a blue shirt waved at her. Wistfully, she waved back, watching the light change on the fluttering sails and envying the sunburned crew seated in the cockpit.

She could still smell the odor of the sickroom on her hands, and hear the voice of her mother calling fretfully from the king-size bed. Her mother had been dying of cancer for almost nine months and her once-beautiful face was raddled with suffering and wasted with disease and her lovely hair as sparse and wispy as thistledown.

Robin tried not to think about her as she ran on past the apartment houses.

Yet the images kept coming, and the all-pervading sadness that filled her days and nights. Ever since Marya's disappearance there had been no end to the underlying melancholy of every house they lived in, every city they went to, and even every picture that her mother had managed to make. Her mother was famous. She had become what people called "a worldwide celebrity," and her last picture about a martyred French nun in

World War II had not only won her an Oscar and made her millions, it had established her as one of the great actresses of the world.

But what good had it done her?

What good were her sables, her jewels—and her three husbands?

She still grieved for Marya as though it had been yesterday instead of eighteen years ago that she had run through the zoo plaza in her high heels and bouffant hairdo, frantically looking for her precious baby daughter.

Robin remembered it vividly . . . the police with their endless questions, the reporters camping outside the apartment, her father constantly pulling his Scottie-dog hair, and her mother walking back and forth in front of the casement windows with her eyes red and a wet ball of handkerchief stuffed against her mouth.

She had watched her mother on TV—clasping her hands with tears running down her cheeks. "Oh—please, friends—if you've seen my baby or know anything about her . . . She's four years old, with long brown hair and big brown eyes—wearing a pink dress and a blue coat and a small gold locket on a chain around her neck. And behind her left ear is a small red birthmark in the shape of a heart . . ."

Later, Robin had gone with her mother on two false alarms—one to Denver in a heavy snowstorm to visit a demented girl of twenty with long brown hair and a strawberry-colored birthmark, and another, two years ago, to the New York City morgue to look at the body of a girl about twenty-three who'd been fished from the waters off Staten Island.

A Lieutenant Feeney, one of the detectives who had worked on Marya's case, led them into a chilly room and pulled open a steel drawer. There, under a coarse sheet, lay the body of a small, slim girl whose shoulder-length dark hair was smoothed back from her bony forehead and whose large dark eyes regarded them with a glassy stare.

Robin heard her mother gasp. Lieutenant Feeney turned

the head gently so that they could see the oddly shaped birthmark, and Robin could feel her mother's long fingernails digging into her arm like claws.

"Is it her?" Lieutenant Feeney asked.

"I—don't know," her mother breathed harshly. "It—it might be . . . it's very like her . . ." She turned to Robin. "What do *you* think, dear?" Her eyes were bright with hope—and horror.

Robin looked into them, then down at the purplish birthmark. It looked nothing like Marya's. "No!" she said firmly. "Let's go, darling." And she dragged her mother from the room.

One year later her mother developed cancer. Privately Robin believed that the stress of her mother's endless anguish had brought it on. In any case, the disease moved swiftly, reducing her mother in a few months' time from a glamorous active woman to a pain-wracked invalid.

Robin's life changed. Since leaving college she had taken over the practical side of her impractical mother's affairs—but now she was not only in charge of her investments, her royalties, her bills, and her fan mail, but she also took care of her mother when her nurse was off duty. In fact there were few moments in the day that she had free, so the hours spent running were especially precious.

The wide promenade curving above the speeding traffic and the river racing below merged into a charming green park leading to Gracie Mansion, the mayor's official residence. Within the park, before one reached the mansion, there was a prettily landscaped area on the left where a flight of steps led down to a bronze statue of Peter Pan set in a small plaza surrounded by greenery.

There she would often stop to rest before making the circuit back to her home on Sutton Place. She loved the boy's delicate features and his dreamy serenity as he sat in his belted tunic with a feather in his cap.

Surrounding him were four small woodland creatures, a

fawn, a rabbit, a bird, and a frog, and sometimes she would give one of them an affectionate pat before starting off again.

It was the kind of thing that Marya would have done, and inevitably Robin would think of her with sadness in that quiet secluded spot, where magic seemed to linger and lost children were forever young.

Then one day in late May she heard a voice behind her.

"Well—hello," he said.

Startled, she turned and stared.

He was sitting on a bench smiling at her—a blond man in blue running shorts and a blue-and-white-striped shirt.

He rose. "Sorry. I didn't mean to scare you."

"You didn't. It's just usually so quiet here," she said.

"Do you come here often?"

He was good-looking, clean-cut, with magnificent muscular legs—the legs of a runner, fuzzed with thick golden hair.

"Fairly often," Robin answered. "It's a good place to catch your breath."

He smiled. "You didn't seem to be out of any when you came down those stairs. You a regular?"

"Pretty much," she said.

He frowned. "How is it I've never seen you?" His voice was soft, with a Southern accent. "I run every chance I get. Whenever I'm in the city. Do you always run this early?"

Robin nodded. "If I can . . . it's the best time . . . the least crowded." Meanwhile, she was noticing his sun-bleached shock of hair and the brightness of his blue eyes in the tanned, handsome face.

"I prefer the morning too . . . and particularly the East Side." He glanced at her legs. "I don't go much for the West Side. It's too broken up."

"I agree."

"How many miles do you do in a morning?"

Robin told him. He looked impressed. They had started

up the steps leading to the upper level of the park. He paused at the top and asked rather wistfully, "I suppose you're planning to hit the pavement again.".

"I have to." She smiled. "I live thirty blocks away."

"God, I wish I could go with you, but I'm expecting a phone call at my hotel in fifteen minutes."

He thrust out his hand, and she offered him her own.

"Well, nice to have met you. My name's Andy Forrester. I'm from Washington, D.C. What's yours?"

"Robin Chodoff."

"Well, Robin Chodoff, it's been a pleasure." His grip was warm and powerful. For a second he looked into her eyes. Then he started off, but immediately came back. "Look. The hell with the phone call. They can try again. Would you care for some breakfast?"

She said yes. And thus began a romance that ran like wildfire through dry grass. By her second cup of coffee she was in love.

Andy Forrester (born Luke Andrew Forrester) wasn't anything like the other men she had known.

He wasn't married or in show biz. He was a lawyer who'd been born on the Eastern Shore of Virginia "in an old white house with pillars and a veranda" and had graduated from the University of Virginia, "where all the Forresters have gone since Thomas Jefferson founded it." He had gotten his law degree at Northwestern University.

"By the time I graduated from UVA I felt I had to get out of the South, much as I love the place. You ever been to the Eastern Shore?"

"No," she said. She hadn't even heard of it.

"Well, it's unique, or it was in my boyhood. Towns like Crisfield, Accomac, Princess Anne, and Chincoteague. They have a special flavor . . . like no other towns in America."

His family were dead, except for an old great-aunt living in Baltimore. "I'd love you to meet her. Old Great-Aunt Violet will probably bore you silly telling you about the Forrester family, but she's a real grand gal, still a tiger at ninety, with an ear for dialect and a wonderful sense of humor."

Robin loved hearing him talk in his soft, easy fashion. She loved the atmospheres he conjured up. They were so different from her own.

After breakfast they met for dinner that same night.

He chose an old-fashioned restaurant in Little Italy, a place where candles were stuck in Chianti bottles, and you could actually order ravioli and not get sneered at. "Nothing trendy." He grinned. "Strictly 1950s. I just happened to stumble into it." There was even an outdoor garden with trellises and vines and an accordion player.

The evening was warm, the air soft and balmy. They sipped Chianti and spoke little—letting the music flow over them and the guttering candles create magic. He found her hand across the table. He pressed it with his warm strong fingers and she felt the calluses on his palms rubbing against her flesh. "You're a find yourself, Robin," he said in his soft voice, husky with emotion. "I've never met a girl like you—one so sweet and unassuming and yet so gorgeous, so exotic. I love your hair." She wore it loose that evening, flowing like a jet-black mantle around her plain white linen dress, and she could see his blue eyes glistening in the candlelight as though he wanted to caress every strand.

They danced cheek to cheek like an old-fashioned couple to the languid Neopolitan tunes, then they walked back to her apartment house on Sutton Place swinging hands and singing some of the songs the accordionist had played.

Outside the locked doors of the lobby he kissed her and held her in his powerful embrace. Then he let her go and watched her cross the lobby after Gus, the security guard, unlocked the front door and let her in. She felt guilty about not asking him up for a drink, but her mother might still be awake and it was too early to tell her anything.

Her mother, who had nothing but her illness to think about, would undoubtedly magnify this romance beyond reason.

Besides, she wanted time to assess her own feelings about this man who had come into her life so suddenly. Andy was very different from the men she had known, the actors and agents and other show-business types, who, she suspected, had cultivated her more for her connections than real love. Andy came from another world entirely, a world she had envied but never really known. And yet he had picked her without knowing anything about her. He liked her for herself perhaps, and her heart, so long starved for love and companionship, welled up inside her in spite of her wariness that he might never call her again, he'd been bored by her company, he was just a Washington playboy killing time on a business trip.

Andy went back to Washington the following morning. He was a government lawyer with the National Park Service and had to travel a great deal. He lived in an apartment on Connecticut Avenue and had given her his address and phone number. By the afternoon of that same day he had phoned her twice, once from his office and again at dusk from his flat. Their second conversation lasted an hour and a half.

He didn't know when he'd be back in New York, goddamn it. There were meetings he had to attend, congressmen he had to see. But at ten the following morning the buzzer sounded from the lobby and Victor the doorman said over the intercom that a huge flower arrangement had arrived downstairs. "For you, Miss Chodoff. Shall I bring it up?"

It was a gorgeous display of peach roses and black orchids. Even Robin's mother was impressed. "It's been ages since I've seen black orchids," she said. "And *peach* roses! Who is he?"

"Oh, somebody from the bank," Robin lied, having hidden the card, "who's trying to interest me in a new investment program." That same afternoon Andy called person to person, and asked her if she could possibly come to Washington for the weekend.

"I can arrange to have you stay with friends, if your mother's worried about the proprieties."

Robin didn't tell her mother about his invitation either, but pretended that an old schoolmate was getting married and wanted her to be a bridesmaid.

"But how inconsiderate of her," said her mother, "asking you this late. What will you do about a dress?"

"She said she'd get me one—probably from the bridesmaid she asked originally. But it sounds like fun, Mumsie—and I won't be gone long. You'll have Suzanne" (Suzanne was the Swiss nurse) "and Marianne and Rose" (the cook and housemaid) "and I'll call you every day to see how things are."

"Well, all right," said her mother in a tone she was trying to keep from sounding aggrieved. "I know I shouldn't be selfish. You've been absolutely nowhere for months and you need a change from this awful house."

"It's not awful and I love you." Robin bent to kiss her, smelling the odor of decay and death. "If you're good I'll bring you back a surprise."

"I don't *want* any surprises. I've had *enough* surprises!"

On Friday afternoon Robin took the shuttle to Washington and Andy met her at National Airport. In his tan raincoat and dark-blue suit he had come directly from the office, and with his attaché case and big black umbrella he looked the picture of a young Washington executive.

It was raining, and huddled under the umbrella, they ran through the downpour to a distant parking lot. As they drove out of the airport, he drew her to him and kissed her so passionately they almost ran into an exit sign.

"God, girl, how I've missed you!"

"Me too," she murmured.

"I couldn't concentrate on my work this morning. I must have messed up a dozen reports."

His hand moved to her knee and rested there, and she felt a thrill that was almost agony as she waited for it to move farther up her skirt.

But it didn't. As they sped along the crowded beltways

he said, "Listen, I'm afraid my friends couldn't make it. Their little boy is sick, and they think it might be catching."

"Oh dear, I'm sorry to hear that."

"They're probably overreacting, but could you, would you, be willing to spend the night in my apartment? It would be more convenient and we'd have more time together."

She hadn't believed a word about the friends and their sick little boy, in fact, from the beginning, she had known that the "friends" were a ruse. It was a line he had given her to use on her mother and she was amused and delighted to have her surmises confirmed. All she wanted was a gala weekend, a break in the monotony of her life since her mother's illness. For a long time there'd been no dates, no parties, only nights and weekends looking at television.

His apartment was in a large, old-fashioned apartment house, a bleak cement pile surrounded by straggly shrubbery. He parked the car in an underground garage and they went up to the seventh floor in a self-service elevator, with only the sound of the creaking machinery and his dripping umbrella to break the silence.

Down a long dim hall that smelled of fried onions he led the way to a door at the far end. Turning the key in a series of locks and bolts, he grinned ruefully. "I'm afraid you won't find it much to look at . . . it lacks a woman's touch. Since no woman's been in it since I moved here."

As the door slammed shut, he grabbed her and held her. "No one but you—*ever!*" he murmured, and gave her a long deep kiss. His hand cupped her breast.

The apartment was small, with a living room, bedroom, a kitchenette, and bathroom, but all she remembered of that weekend was the bedroom. Most of her visit was spent there, in a golden haze of sensuality.

She had feared that Andy might be stuffy and inhibited. She had put him down as an amateur at lovemaking. He turned out to be a master.

Lying on the beige coverlet of the double studio couch,

he was tender and considerate. He made love to her slowly, with gentle caresses of her breasts, belly, and thighs, and seemed to revel in her enjoyment without letting his own needs intrude. After leading her slowly through the stages of arousal, he knew exactly when she was ready for the coup de grâce.

All that afternoon and evening they never left the couch, and at midnight, naked and flushed, they got up and raided the refrigerator. He had stocked it with cold cuts and salads from the deli. He opened a bottle of excellent champagne and they drank every drop and ate every last morsel of the greasy roast beef and the mayonnaise-clogged salads. She had never been so happy. In the cracked bathroom mirror her radiant flushed face and serene gray eyes, with the long black hair tumbled about her naked shoulders, gazed back at her like a mermaid's from the sea.

Back they went to their twisted coverlet, slept for an hour or two, and woke before dawn to the smooth entwined warmth of each other's naked bodies.

Their room, shaded by blinds and hedged in by the rain, reminded her of a cave on a hilltop, some dim, ancient place of sacrifice and orgy where the gods demanded incessant love rituals in return for eternal youth and desire.

She felt drugged by lust. Memory did not exist, nor conscience, nor a sense of time. The bedclothes slid to the floor and they lay writhing, glued together on the stained, lumpy mattress. Her hair swept the dusty carpet, and he perched on his knees above her, like a god riding a wild horse. Or their positions were reversed. She rode *him* like a maenad with arched back and streaming hair poised on a pinnacle of rock, a molten volcano.

They spoke little. They communicated mostly in moans or fierce whispers. She heard the church bells ringing on Sunday morning and it was as though she were hearing the sunken chimes of Debussy's "Cathédrale Engloutie." The rain ended at one, and they drove down to Georgetown and had brunch in a noisy French restaurant. She had hoped to meet his Great-Aunt Violet and he had said something about driving her to Baltimore for tea, but when the meal was finished, they were both much more eager to get back to the apartment and strip off their clothes.

"Andy!" She sat up with a start at six o'clock. "I've got to get home. I'm late as it is."

"Why?" he murmured, kissing her neck. "Stay another night."

"I can't."

She told him about her mother. She hadn't said much about her life until then. But now, feeling that she and Andy were practically one flesh, she blurted out the full details of her past, from the time of Marya's kidnapping to the verdict of her mother's doctors.

"Oh, you poor kid. What you've suffered!" He held her close and stroked her hair.

"I want to marry you," he whispered. "I love you so much, Robin. I want to save your life."

2

ROBIN BROKE THE NEWS to her mother the following day. She apologized for having lied about the bouquet and her school-mate's wedding, and confessed that she had fallen in love with this marvelous lawyer she had met while running. He had asked her to marry him.

Her mother listened in silence.

Lying on the terrace in the shade of a flowering tree, she was dressed in a flowing silk gown of a gay design, and on that breezy morning, amidst the exquisite spring planting—the tulips and daffodils and draped profusion of wisteria—she reminded Robin of a butterfly with broken wings that had fallen on the roof of the building and could not flutter away.

Finally she spoke.

"This is—*very*—interesting," she said in a measured tone, "but why didn't you tell me about him before?"

"Because I wanted to get to know him first. I wanted to be sure of how I felt." Robin reached forward and took her mother's hand in hers. The hand was cold, and on one finger was a huge loose diamond ring. "And I'm crazy about him. I've never felt this way about anyone."

"You said that about Richard," her mother said, referring

to a disastrous love affair Robin had had with an aging actor.

"Oh, he's nothing like Richard!" cried Robin vehemently. "He's young. Good-looking. Well educated—and *nice!* You'll adore him. He's just your type."

"Ah, what *is* my type?" Her mother rolled up her eyes in a mocking way. "I've tried so many in my day."

"I mean, he's not an artist. He's stable, steady, dependable . . . sort of like Uncle Harry . . . a man you can rely on."

Uncle Harry was her mother's older brother—an accountant, long deceased.

"Well, you couldn't do better than Uncle Harry," said her mother. She sighed. "So when do I meet—this paragon of perfection?"

"Very soon—I hope."

"How soon?"

"He said he would phone me this afternoon to hear your verdict."

"Did he? Well, I'm not a judge or a jury. And you've accepted him. So—why does he need *me?*"

"Oh, Mother. You know I'd never marry him without your consent."

"Good heavens, child. You're twenty-six!" Her mother grimaced, and Robin sensed a gleam of triumph in the violet eyes. "So—what if I refuse?"

Robin withdrew her hand from her mother's cold fingers. She gazed across the terrace at the skyscrapers glittering in the bright morning sun.

"I suppose," she said stiffly, "I'll just live with him until you give in."

"Oh, Robin—oh you poor baby." Her mother's voice went caroling across the terrace. And her mother laughed, a soft joyous laugh. "What a charming concession. But I have a better plan."

"What is it?"

"Why don't you wait until I'm dead and gone?" her mother asked almost cheerily. "It won't be long, you know—

and then you'll have everything—my house, my fortune, and your wonderful young man."

"Oh—*Mother!*"

But the interview ended. Suzanne was bringing lunch.

Andy came on Wednesday evening. He arrived half an hour early, and Robin, much flustered, took him out on the terrace and fixed him a Scotch and water while her mother finished dressing.

It was dusk, and the lights were coming on all over the city. The skyscrapers were like giant computers dotted with flashing signals in columns and squares. On the freshly watered terrace the Venetian lanterns had been lit, and they cast a mysterious, soft glow on the pots of daisies, the brick walks, and the massed azaleas, which were just coming into bloom.

"What a perfectly marvelous place . . . it's a palace." Sipping his drink, he strolled about, admiring the antique iron furniture and statuary. He looked wonderful in his dark-blue blazer and gray trousers with his blond hair freshly cut and his face glowing with health. "Have you had it long? What a view. I don't think there's a view like this in the entire city."

Far below, the trafffic swished with a sound like distant surf, and the river curved beyond, all spangled bridges and dancing reflections. They held hands, and in the shadow of the curving brick wall that surrounded the terrace they embraced, a long, bone-crushing embrace that set her body aflame. Again she felt the delirious sensation of his smooth hot lips moving across her mouth and the exciting intrusion of his tongue. He plunged his hand down inside her dress and manipulated her nipples, and in fact had already slid his other hand underneath her skirt and inside her panty hose when the silhouette of Suzanne appeared behind the glass doors of the living room.

Hastily, they rearranged themselves as Suzanne stepped out on the terrace.

"Mademoiselle—?" She looked around. "Your mother is ready."

Robin smoothed her hair and checked her bodice, and they went into the lamp-lit library.

"Would you care for another drink?" she asked.

"No thanks." He grinned. "I think I'd better stay sober for this."

Soon they could hear a footstep and the rustle of chiffon skirts. Haloed by the golden glow of the hallway's indirect lighting, her mother "made an entrance," walking slowly, measuredly, as though a whole theaterful of people were waiting.

Suzanne had done a truly marvelous job. She wore a long navy-blue chiffon dress with a high neck and long sleeves to conceal her ravaged neck and arms. Her only jewelry was a diamond pendant as big as a strawberry, a gift from one of her unlamented husbands, a Beverly Hills psychiatrist. Covering her poor balding head was a thousand-dollar wig, fluffed up and tendriled and swirled in a careless way just as her real hair had once been worn. Framed by its luxuriance, her features looked exquisite, her makeup artful, and her eyes bright and sparkling. Etched with mascara and fringed with false lashes, they resembled a pair of amethysts as she looked up into Andy's eyes with a long look and held out her hand.

"Hello. Is this Andy—the famous Andy—at long last?"

She drawled it in her best manner. She was being phony and Andy was clearly thrilled, although intimidated. Robin could see him looking panicky but forcing a smile as he tried to right himself in the presence of a great actress and coquette, a phenomenon he had probably never encountered in his life.

"Please sit down, Mr.—er—er—Mr. . . ."

"Forrester," he murmured.

"Forrester. I beg your pardon. I'm terrible at names." She had already taken her place on the red velvet loveseat in a corner of the library, and was patting the spot next to her. "Please sit down next to me. I want to see you close up."

As Andy sat down, she smiled bewitchingly, cocked her head to one side, and studied him intently. "Do you know you're very much like that handsome devil Robert Redford . . . and then again you remind me of a man who used to play in German horror films. I forget his name—but maybe you have seen him. He was awfully good . . . back in the thirties."

"I don't recall him, ma'am." Andy smiled politely. "I'm not much for foreign films."

"Well, it doesn't matter. You look more like Robert Redford, whom I positively adore, although I never did a film with him. I wanted to, but my agent wouldn't let me. He felt that Redford was too *wholesome* for the role of a German spy."

"Was that the picture about the French nun?" Andy started to say, but she didn't answer his question, just kept looking at him as though he were some producer she was trying to vamp and get the better of at the same time. It was a look that Robin had often witnessed, and it chilled her to the bone.

Finally, after several more anecdotes about Hollywood and agents in general, her mother fingered the diamond pendant, and asked in a casual tone, "So what's this I hear about you two getting married?"

Andy reddened perceptibly. He took a gulp of his drink. "We'd very much like to, ma'am," he said from deep in his chest.

"You would?" She said it lightly. "And how soon?"

He stared into his glass and then looked over at Robin. "Well—just as soon as Robin's willing," he said. "As far as I'm concerned, I'd like it to be tomorrow."

"*Tomorrow?*"

"Or by the end of the week—at the latest," he said hastily. "I mean—you see, ma'am—I travel a lot in my job—from park to park. Sometimes it's to a battleground from the Civil War or the Revolution, a reenactment of history they're staging for the public. Or there's trouble with campers. Or a forest fire. Or a grizzly kills somebody. That's when they call me, so I can handle the legal side of things . . . the lawsuits."

"How interesting," her mother murmured.

She was watching him from under her black fringe of lashes.

"It *is*." He smiled. "And it takes me everywhere. So—

to get back to the point, ma'am. On Friday of this week—that's two days from now—I'm supposed to fly to Hawaii, where there's a case I can't discuss, but it's on Maui, a particularly beautiful island. I thought it would be nice to take Robin with me—on a well—sort of honeymoon."

"How—lovely."

"Yes, ma'am." He cleared his throat. "We'd be there for about three weeks."

"Three *weeks*?"

Her mother's eyes widened. Ominously.

"Or maybe less," he said quickly. "In any case I thought that maybe we could run down beforehand to city hall or some justice of the peace and have a quiet ceremony."

"Why don't you just go away together without a wedding?" her mother interrupted.

"Oh." He stared at her for a long second. Then he smiled, an awkward smile. "I'm afraid that wouldn't be acceptable to either me or my department. You see—I *believe* in marriage, ma'am, and so do my superiors. And I'm afraid they wouldn't take too kindly to my bringing along a girlfriend for three weeks . . . if you know what I mean."

"Oh I do, Andy, I do. I know exactly what you mean. The world is *so* stuffy, particularly the political world," said her mother. "But it also can be a wee bit in a hurry."

She rose—with difficulty.

"Will you excuse me." Her smile was fixed. She thrust out her hand. "It's been so nice—meeting you, Mr.—er—er—" She gazed at him blankly.

"*Forrester*. I'm *so* sorry."

The heavy lashes fluttered. The violet eyes were cold. "Please come back again—sometime."

She rustled out.

Robin and Andy watched her disappear.

They stood silent, motionless, until the bedroom door clicked shut. Then Robin threw her arms around him. She laid her head on his chest.

"Your mother doesn't like me," he muttered.

"Yes she does. She will. It takes time for her to like people."

"She treated me like a fool. She thought I was an idiot."

He withdrew himself from her arms and walked out into the hallway. She could see his shoulders quivering and his fists clenching and unclenching at his sides.

She ran to him. "Please. Maybe—it was just too much for her. . . .The suddenness . . . the whole idea of leaving . . ."

"Then you're not coming to Maui?" He stopped walking and faced her, his eyes ablaze.

"I don't see how I can, darling." Robin faltered. "She's ill . . . I didn't realize it was only two days from now . . . and she's dying. It's not an—ordinary situation."

The fire in his eyes died away to a look of sadness. Reaching out, he took her hand. "OK—sweetheart. I was wrong to expect so much of you." Drawing her close to him, he kissed the top of her head. "All I wanted was to make *you* happy . . . but if it isn't convenient right now I'll just have to—wait."

"Oh, Andy . . . I'm sorry . . . I'd adore to go with you."

"You still have time to change your mind, of course."

He tilted her lips to his and kissed her. When he had let her go, he stepped back and, smiling, fixed his beautiful blue eyes upon her. "I'll be at the hotel until eleven o'clock tomorrow morning—then I have to notify my boss, one way or other, about you."

"I—I'll call you before eleven."

"I love you, Robin," he whispered.

Again he kissed her, a long lingering kiss, and then strode to the private elevator. Torn with conflict, she stood watching him. The elevator door clicked shut.

3

WHEN SHE CALLED ANDY the next morning, he said that he was sorry for having put her in such a bind. "It was much too soon to expect you to go off with me at a moment's notice. But I guess I didn't realize what unique people you are—and how special is your relationship. Well . . . please tell her to forgive me, and I hope to see her when I get back."

"I'll do nothing of the kind. She treated you abominably."

He laughed. "She's a movie star. I liked her. You can also tell her that."

Robin was silent. Then she said sadly, "I'm going to miss you, darling. Will you write me?"

"Of course I will. I'll be moving around from island to island. They've given me some extra assignments, but you'll hear from me, don't worry about that."

"And you'll be gone about three weeks?"

"More or less," he said.

He called her from the airport just before takeoff for San Francisco and Honolulu, and again they exchanged endearments and promises. Robin could scarcely speak for the tears welling in her eyes at the prospect of nearly a month without him. All that night she wept into her pillow and for the next couple of days went around in a trance, scarcely able to concentrate on her daily tasks and too depressed to go for her morning run.

Her mother never mentioned him. And Robin was too proud to ask her opinion. Andy had been a threat to her mother's security from the beginning, and no discussion would change her mother's determination to dislike him. An out-and-out battle might clear the air, but how could one argue with a dying woman?

Meanwhile, every day her mother seemed to grow more discontented.

Nothing pleased her, neither the food, the weather, the news of the day, nor even the tapes of her old films Robin rented from a video store. It was as though, having spurned Andy as a son-in-law, she hated herself, but was too scared to give an inch in his favor for fear of losing whatever ground she had gained that first evening. So to cover up her conflict, she found fault with petty details.

A week passed in this unpleasant atmosphere. To escape it Robin began running again. On the second morning of her round trip to the Peter Pan statue, she returned to the penthouse and found her mother out of bed and waiting for her outside the door of the small private elevator.

Her mother's face was flushed and her eyes bright with excitement. "Darling, the most wonderful thing has happened. I can't believe it. Look what came in the mail."

Holding up the skirt of her mauve satin dressing gown, she hobbled into her bedroom and picked up a letter. "It's from France. I had Suzanne translate it. And it's just amazing. The most fantastic thing."

"Who's it from? What does it say?"

"Just read it, *read* it!" Her mother thrust the letter under Robin's nose. "Sit down. I can't wait to hear your reaction."

Still dressed in her shorts and running shoes, Robin sat in her father's old rocking chair. The letter was in French and the handwriting was large and clear. Her mother hovered next to her, breathing rapidly.

My Dear Madame . . .

I have recently seen your beautiful film about the martyred nun in World War II and admire your beauty and acting very much. You are a true artist like our beloved Sarah Bernhardt and our magnificent Edwige Feuillère, whose performances have always sprung from a keen intelligence and a deep compassion for humanity.

Robin glanced up at her mother's intense expression. "Are you OK?" she asked.

"Perfect. Keep reading."

Recently I read an article in Elle *magazine which said that you had lost a daughter to kidnappers many years ago, and by a curious coincidence I wondered if she could possibly be a young girl living not far from me on the outskirts of my native city, Rouen.*

I don't wish to get your hopes up unduly, but for one thing she is about the age your daughter would be at the present time. This young girl also bears a striking resemblance to you as you looked in the World War II film. Nor does she resemble any member of her own family. Rumor has it that she was adopted in early childhood, although her father insists she is his natural daughter. I shan't bore you with further details, but I feel that if you could just come to Rouen and see her, you would be interested in investigating her background in detail. If so, I would be more than happy to help you, although naturally I don't want to be known as a meddler, and the last thing I would wish to do is interfere between a father and his daughter.

You may write me care of the general post office in Rouen, and meanwhile my good wishes for your health and happiness.

> À bientôt,
> *Émilie Gautier*

Robin read the letter through twice. Folding it in half, she handed it to her mother.

"What's the *matter* with it?" her mother cried, clutching the letter to her bosom.

"Nothing's the matter. I just can't get too excited about some person who doesn't give us her real address. Just care of the general post office! And says she doesn't want to be known as a meddler. She sounds almost as crazy as that girl in Denver."

"I don't agree," her mother answered, looking more and more upset. "Listen, don't you remember that old foreign woman in the park? The one who scared Marya? Well—maybe she was this French woman."

"Nonsense. Why on earth would she write us?"

"She could have stolen Marya and be feeling conscience-stricken."

"Oh, Mother. That old woman was *ancient*. She could scarcely walk!"

Her mother clasped her hands to her breast. Tears sprang into her eyes. "Oh my God," she said. "I was so very happy, and now you've taken all the joy out of it!"

She tottered across the room and flung herself on the bed.

In the fashionable finishing schools Robin attended she had learned to speak and write French almost like a native. It had been her favorite subject. That evening she translated an answer to Émilie Gautier that her mother had composed after she recovered her equilibrium.

In it her mother said that she was grateful for the information and very *very* interested in anything further that Madame Gautier could tell her about the girl. Her mother wanted to include all the details of the kidnapping and describe the old woman who had sat on the park bench, but Robin dissuaded her and also insisted that her mother say nothing about the state of her own health. "There's no need to be personal or get chummy with her. She may be doing it just to attract attention, like all those other celebrity hounds."

Reluctantly, her mother signed the typewritten sheet and Robin walked to the corner mailbox and slipped it through the slot.

Three days passed. Four days—of stewing and tension as mail time approached. On the sixth day a letter arrived in the same large, careful handwriting. Émilie Gautier wrote that she had received madame's kind letter. She appreciated it very much and would call her on the fifteenth of June between the hours of 6:00 P.M and 10:00 P.M. "your time." Evidently piqued by the impersonal tone of her mother's letter, Madame Gautier added that her home address was Pension Bertrand, 18 Rue de Grenoble, Rouen, France, and suggested that if madame wished to investigate her further, she could call Monsieur Raoul Guzman at l'Agence de Détective Privé de Guzman, 4 Avenue Molotoff, Paris, France, and he would supply any credentials desired.

"So there!" Her mother's voice cracked as she looked up from the letter. "She's no fraud. She's intelligent, authentic, and scrupulously honest."

"Do you want me to call this Guzman detective agency?"

"If you wish. I don't think it's necessary."

Robin called. A secretary answered. Monsieur Guzman was not in, but he would return her call, if mademoiselle would leave a phone number.

Robin left it. An hour later Guzman called and asked to speak to her. He was friendly and businesslike. Yes, he knew Madame Gautier personally, and had known her for twenty years. She was a nurse living in Rouen and a personal friend of his mother and his aunt, both of whom she had taken care of during various illnesses.

At six that same evening the telephone rang.

Her mother had been waiting impatiently since five o'clock. Propped on her lace pillows, she picked up the cordless phone.

"Allo . . . bonne nuit . . ." she faltered. "Mais oui . . . un moment . . ." Frantically she gestured to Robin to pick up the extension phone in the library and handle the conversation, for her own French was limited to a few schoolgirl phrases.

Robin hurried into the library and picked up the phone. Madame Gautier's voice was hoarse and deep. "*Vous ne parlez pas français?*" she was asking Robin's mother.

"*Un peu . . . malement . . .*" her mother's voice was quavering. "Robin, are you there? *Ma fille parle avec vous.*"

"*Vous avez une autre fille?*"

Restraining a giggle, Robin came on. "May I help you, Madame Gautier?" she said smoothly in French. "I'm Robin, her older daughter." Deliberately she swallowed her *r*'s and sounded a touch more nasal than necessary.

"Ah. *Très bien. Bon soir.* I have some news for you."

Madame Gautier said that there was "some emergency in the situation," since she had recently learned that the girl and her father were planning to leave France for Martinique in a week or so.

"You mean that she won't be available in a week or so?"

"*Peut-être.* So I think if your mother is coming, she should act promptly," said Madame Gautier.

"But she can't come at all," Robin said.

"*Comment, mademoiselle?* What did you say?"

"She's very ill. She's been sick for several months. Bedridden. And unable to travel."

"*Quel dommage,*" gasped Madame Gautier, as though she had just fallen through a ceiling. "But why didn't you tell me?"

"I'm sorry," Robin said. "Could you perhaps send us a photograph?"

There was a brief silence. "Madame Gautier, are you still there?" her mother called anxiously.

"*Oui, madame.* But I cannot send a photograph."

"Why?" asked Robin.

"None is available. And she is too well guarded. Chaperoned—constantly. So the only way is to come in person and regard her face to face."

"Oh dear." From the cordless phone came a despairing sigh.

"I'm afraid that's impossible," Robin said quickly. "But thank you very much, madame, for letting us know about her."

"Then your mother isn't coming?"

"She *can't.*"

"Very well," came the answer in a rather huffy tone. "Then I'm sorry, mademoiselle. I have troubled you in vain. *Hélas.* It is a pity . . . for she is the very image of your beautiful mother . . . and perhaps your sister."

The connection to France was broken off.

When Robin went into her mother's bedroom, her mother was lying face down, sobbing into her pillows.

She sat on the bed and tried to take her mother in her arms. She told her mother that she was sure Madame Gautier would call again—for the French woman had obviously contacted them for some ulterior motive and would not give up easily.

Her mother refused to listen. She continued to sob.

"Look," Robin said, "I'd go over there myself. I remember Marya perfectly . . . but I think it would be a mistake."

Her mother rolled over on her back.

"Why is it a mistake? She's your sister," she whimpered. "Is anything a mistake that might possibly bring her back?"

Her mother's face was swollen with weeping. Tears were coursing down her thin cheeks.

"Of course it isn't . . . but try to be reasonable. The possibility that this girl is Marya is terribly remote. It's one chance in a million. And if she's so well guarded, even *seeing* her may be difficult. Besides—if you were this girl's father, would *you* want some stranger poking around in your private life? You'd hate it—and you know how the French people are . . . *fearfully* private and suspicious."

"Oh, why are you so mistrustful and cynical?" her mother wailed, falling back on her pillows again. "Oh, this cursed, cursed illness!" She closed her eyes and turned her head back and forth as though she were in pain. "If I were well, I'd be on a plane right now. I wouldn't be scared of some stupid Frenchman. I'd go straight to Mitterrand."

"Nonsense. We must be reasonable."

"What was reasonable about that kidnapping?"

Robin did not reply. She rocked in the old rocker, the first Christmas present her mother had given her father. She thought of how he had sat in it after Marya disappeared, smoking cigarettes and pulling at his shaggy black hair.

"I agree, Mother. Nothing is reasonable. We've lived a kind of improvised life for years—ever since she disappeared." Sadly she looked across the bed into her mother's tear-filled eyes. "If I thought I could change our luck by going to France and seeing this girl, I'd go in a flash—but the thing is, Mumsie darling . . ."

She rose and walked over to the French doors leading to the terrace, and looked toward the brick wall where Andy had kissed her.

"The thing is . . . ?" her mother was asking.

Robin turned. "The thing is that I don't trust this damned woman or understand her motives. Why is she so *bent* on bringing this girl to your attention?"

"Because—she's a fan of mine . . . she admires me— and pities me."

Robin shrugged. "Is she just a lonely neurotic with a wild imagination? Or does she expect money for every bit of information she furnishes? Or is her motive revenge on the girl's father? Or will she demand a big sum for merely revealing the girl's name and address?" She moved toward the bed. "And furthermore, why is there such a big hurry about it? She didn't mention this Martinique business before. Mother—you've got to *think* of such things before getting involved."

"I *have* thought of them, and I still think we should trust her. Didn't that Guzman person say she was legitimate?"

Robin was silent. She walked back to the glass doors.

"You just don't want to go look for Marya?" her mother said softly. "Is that it?"

Robin turned and faced her. "Of course I don't. I don't want to leave you. Didn't I prove that a week ago?"

"You mean—with that young man?" Her mother sniffed. "This isn't the same thing. It wouldn't take you more than a couple of days. You could fly over, see the girl, and fly right back. All I'm asking from you is one look at her."

"It might take much longer than a couple of days."

"And it might *not*." Her mother's voice rose imperiously. Her eyes flashed. After a pause she asked in an accusing tone, "Or don't you *want* your sister back?"

Her voice rang through the darkening room. Robin stared at her, a long, shocked look. Then she walked to the bed. She picked up the cordless phone.

"I'd like to make an overseas call," she said. "Person to person. To a Mrs. Émilie Gautier. At the Pension Bertrand, Eighteen Rue de Grenoble, in Rouen, France."

4

JUST BEFORE she flew to Paris Andy called from Honolulu.

His voice was faint, and queer beeps and clicks kept interrupting their conversation, but she was so glad to hear his voice that the bad connection didn't matter.

He was fine. He missed her, even though he'd been on the go ever since he'd arrived. There had been a lot of conferences on a new state park that was just being developed, and a two-day trip to an extinct volcano on a remote island reached only by an outrigger canoe.

"But how've *you* been, darling? What have you been up to?"

She told him about France and Madame Gautier's letter, expecting him to be skeptical, but he sounded rather hopeful.

"It's possible," she heard him say between buzzes and whines in the equipment. "Missing people *have* been found on occasion. Look at Livingstone."

"Who?"

"Livingstone, the explorer. So—how long will you be gone?"

"I have no idea," she shouted over static.

"Where can I reach you?" His voice came faintly, then loudly. "Where will you be staying?"

"I'm not sure. But you can probably reach me at the Pension Bertrand on the Rue de Grenoble."

"What? What's that . . . ?

"Number eighteen—Pension—Bertrand—on the Rue de Grenoble."

She finally had to spell it. He didn't know a word of French. "Well—OK," he said, sounding deeply exasperated. "Thanks, darling. And good luck. I'll do my best to get through to you. And—chin up. Think what it would mean to us."

"Us?"

"Good Lord." She heard his deep hearty chuckle over thousands of miles. His voice was clear suddenly. "With your sister on the scene, she'd forget all about us . . ."

There was more, but it was garbled, and finally she hung up.

She flew to Paris aboard the Concorde and landed at De Gaulle. From there she took a cab north to Rouen. The ride took about an hour up a drab superhighway crowded with small speeding cars and trucks. Halfway there it began to rain and all her notions of picturesque Normandy were blotted out by mist and a thunderstorm.

She had never been to Rouen. She had heard that it was very old and noted for its religious austerity and provincialism. It was the city where Joan of Arc had been burned as a witch. Glancing out the window as her taxi crossed the Seine, she glimpsed the tall spires of cathedrals, cobblestoned streets, and blocks of antique houses with peaked roofs and timbered walls. The driver told her that most of them were reproductions of houses dating from the fourteenth century that had been bombed "by your Allied airmen" during World War II.

He had to get out a map and ask directions several times before they came upon the Rue de Grenoble, which was at the head of a long, narrow alley dividing two large, windowless stone buildings. At the far end of the alley, in a kind of cul-de-sac flanked by a high brick wall, was a small square edifice pockmarked with age and resembling a stable or an old-fashioned garage.

"That must be it, mademoiselle."

"*Mon Dieu*," Robin said. "There must be a mistake."

There wasn't. In faded black lettering the name BERTRAND was visible on the front wall of the square building. There seemed to be no windows, only a cavelike front entrance leading in from the street.

"Are you *sure* this is it?"

"There's no other Rue de Grenoble," the driver said. "It's an old city with old streets, some of them like alleys."

Just as she was getting out of the cab with her duffel bag, a tall woman came hurrying up. "*Excusez-moi*, are you Mademoiselle Chodoff?"

The hoarse voice was familiar. "*Bonjour*," said the lady, baring large, prominent teeth. "I am Émilie Gautier. Welcome to Rouen."

She wore a long navy-blue cape and a white nurse's cap perched on frizzy red hair. "I am sorry to be late. I had a case across the city, an emergency, *hélas*. Otherwise I had intended meeting your plane. How is your dear mother? And how was your flight?" Hooking her arm through Robin's and attempting to carry the duffel bag, she led the way to the front door of the building. Her manner was as effusive as though they'd known each other for years.

They went up stone steps into a dank, grimy tunnel, which led to an iron gate Madame Gautier unlocked. Beyond the gate was a stone passageway leading to a glass door that she pushed open, and inside the glass door was a minuscule, shadowy lobby.

"Welcome to the Pension Bertrand!" Madame Gautier waved her hand over an array of shabby tables and chairs. "It goes back to the thirteenth century." A bare wooden counter ran across one end of the room and on the opposite side a rather shaky-looking iron staircase wound its way to some unseen upper floor.

"You *are* staying here, I hope. It will be so much more convenient. And *cheap*!" She flashed her prominent teeth in a smile. "I've made your reservation with Madame Voisin, our concierge, in any case, and as soon as she returns from church we'll register you. *D'accord?*"

"*D'accord*," said Robin politely. The Pension Bertrand looked dismal at first glance, but in their second phone conversation Madame Gautier had highly recommended its good food and friendly atmosphere, and said that the young girl who looked like Marya came there every day with her father for breakfast.

"Let's go up to my room, where we can have some privacy." Madame Gautier led the way up the winding iron staircase. A bleak corridor of whitewashed plaster lay at the head of the stairs. Ancient doors, all with enormous keys dangling from their locks, stretched along the hallway. The air was chilly. But Madame Gautier's room was warm and rather elegant in the light of a shaded lamp, with its mahogany sleigh bed, dark-red silk curtains, gilt-framed oil paintings, and worn Oriental rug.

"Sit down, *chérie*." She motioned Robin to a Louis Quinze chair done in faded green damask. "Would you care for some wine? A cigarette, *peut-être?*" Pulling a pack of Gaulois from the bosom of her white uniform, she laughed hoarsely. "I know it's unhealthy, but I confess I can't part with my leetle husband so easily." Looking at the cigarette affectionately, she tapped it on the back of her hand and stuck it into her mouth. "Even though it may kill me, I need tobacco like I need a man."

With the cigarette bobbing from her thick scarlet lips, she unclasped the nurse's cloak and tossed it on the bed. Then, carefully, she removed the bobby pins from her starched cap and preened before the mirror, fluffing up her hair. It was thin and dry-looking, hennaed a rusty shade after the fashion of many middle-aged French women. Madame Gautier was probably about fifty-five, with a fairly slim body and a graceful walk. But her face reminded Robin of a horse. No amount of cosmetics could conceal the long square jaw, the prominent nose with its large nostrils, and the small close-set eyes with their look of anxiety.

As she turned and tilted her head in the lamplight, pulling a bottle of wine and two glasses from a cupboard and then producing a small plate of madeleines, she seemed extraordinarily nervous and overanxious to please.

"And *how* is your beautiful mother? What a lovely lady." She perched on the edge of the bed, puffing out cigarette smoke and fixing her intent gaze on Robin, who sat sipping wine. "I hope she's feeling better, in fact much improved by our good news. I heard somewhere that she has cancer—*n'est-ce pas?*—but I've known many cancer patients who've recovered completely once they regained their will to live."

"I wish my mother could be that lucky."

"Ah. I pray that too. *Pauvre femme.* How much she has suffered. How *tragique* for someone so talented, so *exquise . . .*" She drew deep on her cigarette. "But be hopeful, Mademoiselle Chodoff. I feel sure you're going to be very glad you came."

They talked about the girl, whose name was Irène. "She is *supposedly* the daughter of a Count Edouard d'Egremont, a minor member of the nobility with very little money and a very bad temper. He was known to beat his wife and probably caused her death five years ago of a so-called heart attack, though a doctor of my acquaintance said there were bruises on her body. In any case, the only person in the world he seems fond of is that child. That Irène. He guards her like a dragon."

She told Robin how she had first become interested in the girl.

In the late 1970s she had been sent on a case involving an old woman living alone in a small, nondescript house deep in the woods.

"She was about eighty years old and had lived alone for many years. Nobody knew much about her, except that she had come to Normandy, bought the house, and furnished it elegantly, but never entertained or mingled with the local people. She was foreign, with an unpronounceable name that even now I can't remember—but *alors*, she had been taken ill and needed a nurse.

"I took care of her for about a week. Toward the end she became delirious. And one night I heard her asking God to forgive her a terrible sin.

"I heard her talking about a city—and a lake far over the sea. And a little child like an angel whom she had seen walking near the lake and snatched up on impulse. Fleeing through the streets and pacifying its cries with candy, she had taken it to her room in the city and pretended it was her granddaughter. But soon fear set in and she decided to take passage on a ship bound for Europe, traveling in steerage, and telling the people the child was her dead daughter's little girl.

"I gathered that most of the time during the voyage the child was ill."

Robin drew in her breath.

Whether true or false, the story made her cringe.

"And then what happened?"

"I'm not perfectly clear," Madame Gautier replied, "but by the time the ship landed she had long since regretted the kidnapping and decided she must rid herself of the child somehow. In Venice, where she found work as a cook to some rich people, she overheard a wealthy couple from France who were visiting her employers, bemoaning their childlessness and talking about adopting an infant from an orphanage. With some hesitation she found the courage to approach them, and a deal was made. In return for the child they paid her an enormous sum, but made her promise never to see the child again or ever reveal its true identity to anyone."

"I can see their point," Robin murmured.

"I suppose so . . . but it was immoral, and perhaps cruel to the old woman," said Madame Gautier with a flash of her dark eyes. She stubbed out her cigarette in an ashtray heaped with butts. "But now let me tell you how I made the connection from my dying patient to the d'Egremont family."

Pulling out another cigarette from her limp pack, she lit it and inhaled deeply for a second.

"It was, if you ask me," she said, at last resuming her

tale, "a most amazing streak of luck, although it took thinking on my part. In another part of Normandy, on the Channel coast, was the d'Egremont estate. They were very rich people at the time, with many holdings. But they had never had children— until one day, when the Countess d'Egremont was in her late forties, they suddenly showed up with a beautiful little daughter of seven who they said had been born in Switzerland but had been too sickly to bring home until the Swiss doctors cured her."

She smiled.

"Interesting?" she asked with her dark eyes gleaming.

"Very," said Robin.

"Very, indeed. Nobody in Rouen believed that story, of course, although Madame La Comtesse stuck to it till the day she died. We all thought that little Irène was the count's bastard, or maybe the result of some indiscretion on the part of the countess. I myself never suspected who she *really* might be until I took care of the old woman—then saw your mother in that film about the nun and read the article in *Elle* magazine." She touched Robin's sleeve. "But I have never told anyone here of my suspicions, and I hope you won't discuss it with anyone either, for news travels fast up here in Normandy, and we don't want the count, her father, to get wind of it, and make trouble for me. He would of course deny everything. In fact he probably never knew of the old woman's whereabouts, although she must have moved here to be near the child." She smiled broadly. "*C'est ça, Mademoiselle Chodoff.* Are you convinced now, and properly excited?" She squeezed Robin's arm. "You don't think I'm such a four-flusher as you did at first, *d'accord?*" She laughed a deep guttural laugh.

"I never thought you were a four-flusher." Reddening, Robin rose from the Louis Quinze chair. "And I'm to see her tomorrow?"

"*Them.* The father and daughter. They're always together. He watches her like a hawk."

"But they'll be here for breakfast?"

Madame Gautier shrugged.

"I *hope* they'll be here. One never knows—from day to day. But if not tomorrow, then the day after."

"I see."

Madame Gautier studied her for a second. Then she slid off the bed. She took Robin's arm again.

"Don't worry. I wouldn't have brought you here for any other reason." She led Robin to the door. "But come, your room should be ready. Let's go and register with Madame Voisin."

5

MADAME VOISIN was a short, box-shaped woman with white hair. She wore a long black silk dress with a white lace collar and had such red cheeks she resembled a clown.

"We are so happy to have you with us, mademoiselle. How was the weather in New York? May I see your passport, please?" Her voice was low-pitched and breathy, as though it were being smothered by her enormous breasts, which were stuffed into her tightly buttoned dress like loaves of bread.

" Sign here, *s'il vous plaît*." She presented a large black ledger filled with names in many handwritings. "We prefer cash to a credit card but if credit cards are all you have, well, then I'm sure Émilie will vouch for you. She's our *oldest* customer." Her laugh at Madame Gautier's expense was deep and hearty but so wheezy one felt that she might never emerge from it alive. "I mean the longest-staying." She wiped her eyes. "By the way," she wheezed, "your meals are included. At least breakfast and dinner. Breakfast is a *little* breakfast, no orange juice, just rolls and coffee."

"Come on, Louise," said Madame Gautier. "Give her her key. Which room have you given her?"

"Number five, the best in the house."

It was very informal at the Pension Bertrand. "Like a family," said Madame Gautier, leading Robin once more up the winding staircase. "Not many frills but clean and comfortable." She turned number five's huge brass key in the lock and swept open the door. "*Voilà. Très jolie, n'est-ce pas?* It's always been one of my favorites."

It was pitch dark.

A green shade was pulled down to the sill at the one window. When lifted, it revealed a blank wall about three inches beyond the windowpane. But when the two china lamps on either side of the bed were lit, the room took on a certain French charm, with its big brass double bed, large carved mahogany armoire standing against one wall, and small antique desk with a rickety gilt chair to match.

There was no bathroom. The "necessities," as Madame Gautier called them, were taken care of by a large crockery bowl and pitcher and a commode covered by a piece of worn green carpet.

After Madame Gautier had gone, Robin stood shaking her head and laughing ruefully. What a place—and what a tale to tell Andy when he called her up. The Pension Bertrand reminded her of a boardinghouse in a novel of Balzac's and the two ladies she had met were like a couple of his outlandish characters—odd-looking, full of quirks, and about a hundred years behind the times.

A dinner gong sounded in the far-off reaches belowstairs. It was seven o'clock. Three minutes later Madame Gautier knocked. "Coming, *chérie? C'est le dîner,*" she called in her hoarse voice, but Robin had had enough of her for the time being and was too tired to face a roomful of strangers.

"Will you excuse me? I'm exhausted from the jet lag." Opening the door, she smiled a weary smile. Then, shutting it gently, she locked it with the huge brass key. Pulling off her clothes, she crawled into the big soft bed.

* * *

The sheets were pure linen and smelled of the iron. She slept a dreamless sleep, and only woke when another knock sounded.

"*Bonjour, mademoiselle.* Are you awake? It's seven."

"Seven? How could it be?" Robin called from her locked-in darkness. "It isn't *morning*?"

"*Mais oui.* The sun has been up for an hour and a half. And breakfast will soon be served. They start at seven-fifteen and they're out of croissants by seven-twenty." This last was accompanied by a husky chuckle.

Robin dressed in haste while Madame Gautier waited outside in the whitewashed corridor. When Robin emerged, Madame Gautier hooked her by the arm. "Did you sleep well? Is your room comfortable? How was the mattress? Do you need another pillow?"

Robin said that the only thing she missed was a phone in her room. Was there one in the building, a pay phone she could use? Madame Gautier replied that yes, of course, the pension possessed a phone, but it was in the concierge's office, and not available for outgoing calls. "Of course if you *receive* a call, if one comes in for you, Madame Voisin will take the message or send someone to your room to fetch you downstairs to answer it."

"Oh dear," said Robin, finding this arrangement fraught with complications—since neither her mother nor Andy spoke French. "And how about outgoing calls? Can I use her phone to make them?" she asked. "I'll pay her for them, naturally."

"*Mais non, hélas, c'est impossible,*" replied Madame Gautier. Outgoing calls could not be made on Madame Voisin's phone. "She's a wee bit sticky on the subject," said Madame Gautier, rolling up her eyes and drawing down the corners of her mouth. "She's been cheated, you see, in the past, by people who charged enormous bills and didn't pay them, and so she's made these rules, although it isn't fair to *honest* persons like yourself."

By this time they had gone down the stairs and arrived

in the lobby, which looked considerably more cheerful than on the previous overcast day. Sunlight flickered on the white walls and old-fashioned furniture and the open glass doors led to a sunny courtyard decked with pots of geraniums.

"Most of the guests," continued Madame Gautier, "make their outside calls at the telephone exchange."

"And where is that located?"

"Not far. Around the corner."

"Good *morning*, ladies." Red-cheeked and wheezing, Madame Voisin waddled toward them. "Did you sleep well, mademoiselle? Is everything satisfactory?"

"*Oui, madame*," lied Robin politely.

"I'm *so* glad, *chérie*." When Madame Voisin smiled, her small blue eyes almost disappeared into the folds of her bright-red cheeks. "I hope you like it here. Most Americans do. They love the old-world charm and the friendly atmosphere. Did Émilie tell you that we go back to the thirteenth century? But yes. Jeanne d'Arc, God bless her, was not even born when this place was built—as a Trappist monastery. They used to make the most delicious liqueurs—and medicines and cheeses."

"What a bore she is," muttered Madame Gautier as they walked out into the pretty, summery courtyard. "And so overweight. She's going to die if she doesn't cut down on those liqueurs and cheeses . . ."

The dining room was off the courtyard, a small square room with white café curtains and snowy tablecloths. Here and there a few old men and women were seated on bentwood chairs, munching on rolls and sipping coffee.

"I guess most of them have eaten already," whispered Madame Gautier as she chose a table not far from the door. "It's late. I just *hope* we haven't missed them." Leaning forward, she rolled her eyes and said in a meaningful tone, "You know—the mystery couple."

Behind a large square table at the far end of the room stood a tall sour-looking young woman in a white butcher's apron.

She was very pregnant. Next to her stood a little boy with fair hair and the face of an angel.

"*Viens donc!* What are you standing there for?" the pregnant woman snarled at the child.

"*Oh, pardon . . .*" He scurried forward to Robin's table.

He was thin and frail-looking, in skimpy tan short shorts and a faded blue cotton shirt. His big blue eyes had a sad, soulful look. His age could have been anywhere from six to eight.

"What would you like for the breakfast, *mesdames?*" he piped, looking anxiously at Madame Gautier.

"*Café noir* and a roll for me," said Madame Gautier. "No milk and no sugar. Just black. Don't forget."

"*Oui, Madame Gautier,*" he answered humbly. "*Café noir—sans lait, sans sucre.*" He turned to Robin. "*Et que voulez-vous, mademoiselle?*"

"What's your name?" Robin asked in French.

"Jean-Pierre," he answered gravely.

Robin smiled. "That's a beautiful name," she said. "I'll have some coffee with hot milk, and a croissant, if you please."

"I'm sorry, mademoiselle." His blue eyes clouded. "There are no more croissants. There are only the rolls."

She noticed how carefully and precisely he spoke French, as though he were fearful of pronouncing it wrong.

"Then I'll have a roll—a soft one, if possible."

"*Merci, mademoiselle.*" No effort on her part could bring a smile to his pale face.

When he had left she asked Madame Gautier who he was.

"The concierge's grandson," she answered with a sniff. "And that one pouring coffee is his mother, Madame Sophie." She nodded toward the sour-looking woman in the butcher's apron. "God knows who his father is—or who's the father of the new one. She's a real sex fiend."

Madame Sophie, with her washed-out features and skimpy blond hair screwed into pink hair curlers, looked nothing like a sex fiend—nor did she resemble her beautiful little son in the least. In fact she didn't seem to like him. As he stood on tiptoe to relay their order, she glared down at him, then her hand shot out and she boxed him on the ear. Staggering back with a soft cry, he clapped his hand to his head.

What a hateful woman. Robin boiled inside as she stared pityingly at the ethereal blond child and then glowered at the mean-faced mother with her poppy eyes, tight, disgruntled mouth, and belligerent attitude.

Even the way she poured the coffee, slopping it into the white crockery cups, and slapped the two hard rolls down on two crockery plates, seemed expressive of the discontent she felt with her lot in life.

Having indulged her own lust with some fly-by-night ne'er-do-well, she was no doubt taking out her frustration on her wretched little son, who was doing his best to carry the overfilled cups back through the dining room and keep the rolls from falling off the small plates she had set them on.

Robin smiled at him again. "Thank you, monsieur. Everything is perfect."

He gazed up at her unhappily. There were tearstains on his cheeks. "I'm sorry there aren't any soft rolls this morning. *Peut-être* tomorrow there will be some."

As Robin sat listening to this pathetic apology and trying to think of some way to cheer him up, she felt her foot being nudged underneath the table. And looking up, she saw Madame Gautier waggling her hennaed eyebrows and going through all sorts of facial contortions as she gazed toward the door leading in from the courtyard.

The Mystery Couple had arrived.

The man was tall and commanding, with wavy gray hair. He looked like an aristocrat, although he was oddly dressed for a summer morning—in a black Chesterfield overcoat, yellow gloves, and gray striped trousers.

The girl looked even odder. She seemed ethereal, as though from another time. In her severe old-fashioned outfit she reminded Robin of the melancholy heroine in *The French Lieutenant's Woman.*

Bent forward, her face was scarcely visible behind her masses of long hair. She wore a long black cloth coat that came almost to her ankles. Her stockings and shoes were those of a nun, plain, black, and sensible.

Swiftly the two newcomers moved down the other side of the dining room and took a table not far from Robin and Madame Gautier's.

The girl was facing her. After she had finished smoothing back her hair, she unbuttoned her black coat. Robin could get a fairly good look at her.

Her hair was gorgeous, very thick and wavy, and seemed the exact color of Marya's childish hair. Richly brown with golden highlights, it curled around her face in soft tendrils and fell to her shoulders, where some of it was drawn back into a big black ribbon, giving her a look of schoolgirl naïveté.

She looked about twenty-two.

Marya's twenty-second birthday was coming up in August.

Robin kept staring, drinking in details. The resemblance to her mother was startling.

The girl's eyes remained downcast. Her cheeks were turning pink. Obviously she found it painful to be stared at by the people in the dining room. Her entrance had caused a stir and the old folks were craning their necks and whispering to each other over their coffee cups at this beauty who had added glamour to their breakfast.

Marya, as a little girl, had hated being looked at. If someone told her she was pretty she would try to hide behind Robin's skirt.

Suddenly the girl looked up, and their eyes met across the sunlit room. For a long moment they faced each other, and Robin's heart began skipping beats as she gazed into the beautiful brown eyes with their long dark lashes and eyebrows that were pointed on top.

Marya's eyebrows had been pointed on top.

As a child she had had a habit of raising them very high when she was awed by some unusual sight—a huge Easter bunny in a department store or a rat lying dead in a gutter. Her eyebrows, like her mother's, were extremely mobile, weathervanes of her emotions, and Robin kept watching, waiting for them to move.

The brown eyes remained fixed steadily on her, and Robin wondered whether just possibly the girl recognized her.

Then "Irène" lowered her eyes and turned to the little boy, Jean-Pierre, who had appeared at her side to take her order. Her lips moved, her lashes fluttered, as she spoke to the child in a shy, awkward manner. She seemed unusually self-conscious even with someone as timid and uncritical as the boy, and when she turned to her father, Robin could see how slavishly she deferred to him, as though his every word was precious.

Again in this regard she resembled Marya, who had always been dependent, deferential, and obedient. Even at four Marya had been an unusually docile child who defied her parents only once in Robin's memory, by lying down on the sidewalk when she realized she was on her way to the doctor's office. She had always done what she was told to do, without whining or throwing a temper tantrum.

Was Irène Marya?

She appeared to be her mirror image—a grown-up version of her little sister.

Her clothes, for instance, were so out of key with her beauty. No self-respecting young woman would ever have worn that long black coat and old-fashioned serge dress.

Yet Marya grown up might have accepted such garments without question, if her father had picked them out for her. As a child she had had no vanity, but had always accepted anything put on her, whether it fit or it didn't, just as she would eat almost anything set before her. This very quality of acceptance had been a torment to her mother ever since the kidnapping. "Whatever they'll do to her she'll accept without question, and not give a peep," she had said many times after Marya's disappearance, as she paced the apartment on Fifty-seventh Street.

If this *was* really Marya, would she remember Fifty-seventh Street?

After eighteen years of separation from all she'd known, what memories would exist in the brain of a child who'd been only four at the time of the kidnapping?

Would she still retain even a dreamlike recollection of that sunny apartment, the sound of a piano, and the books their father had read to them—*Goodnight Moon* and *Winnie-the-Pooh*—or would it all have been supplanted by images of France?

Robin realized that she was crying. Tears were starting in her eyes. Quickly she stared at the tablecloth, and picking up the paper napkin, held it against her face. But Madame Gautier had noticed. Her small black eyes were gazing across the table, and in them was a gleam of triumph.

The father and daughter were rising from their table.

"*Garçon—l'addition!*" The count snapped his fingers and barked in a commanding tone.

Soon Jean-Pierre came running with a slip of paper in his hand. The count snatched it from him imperiously.

For a long moment he studied the bill. Then, muttering something in a surly tone, he reached into his overcoat pocket, produced a limp wallet, and extracted a worn bank note.

He tossed it at the child. It fluttered to the ground and the little boy stooped and picked it up.

"*Merci, monsieur.*" He beamed and made a little bow.

"I want change," the count barked.

"*Oh, pardon, Monsieur Le Comte . . .*"

Off he ran on his spindly legs while the count stood tapping his foot. Meanwhile, his daughter drooped at his side with an indifferent expression, an air of weariness. Soon the boy returned, and he waited while the tall, hawk-nosed man towering above him counted the coins he had brought him and dropped them in his coat pocket. The count turned on his heel.

"Come, Irène. We're late," he growled. When she did

not move fast enough, he took her by the arm and propelled her toward the courtyard so rapidly she knocked over a chair with her long sweeping coat.

Helplessly she looked back, murmuring an apology, but he swept her out of the dining room, and the pair hastened across the courtyard and disappeared into the lobby.

6

THE SUNLIT CITY of Rouen was like a painting by Monet, with its lacy cathedral spires rising golden from the morning mist and its cobblestones reflecting glistening bits of blue sky.

After breakfast Robin fled from the pension, heading for the Seine and its busy river traffic. Barges passed her, bound for the Channel and moving fast with washing aflutter. Trawlers heavy with fish went by and blue-smocked fishermen waved to her. Now and then a huge tanker swept past in a flurry of foaming swells.

The Seine reminded her of the East River. It was also narrow and green and fierce. She ran beside it as it rushed through the city after its long trip from Paris, and its turbulence seemed to match her tumultuous state of mind. For she could not bring herself to call her mother just yet. She did not know what to tell her.

Should she say that she had perhaps stumbled on a miracle? Or give voice to her doubts that the girl was really Marya? Irène did indeed resemble Marya in many ways, but the likeness could be merely an illusion after the buildup Madame Gautier had given her.

For several miles Robin ran on blindly, seeing little on either side—neither the tour buses, nor the Gothic architecture, the quaint old houses, the medieval banners. Always before her was that lovely face with its haunted brown eyes. Seldom had she seen a face so melancholy, and so lost.

After an hour of steady running, she headed for the telephone exchange.

In a large airy building she gave her mother's number to a girl at a switchboard and stepped into a glass booth to wait for the call to go through.

As she waited she realized that she was wet from head to foot—not so much from running as from the prospect of dealing with her mother's reaction.

Whatever she might say would set her mother's imagination on fire.

The phone began ringing in the booth and she picked up the receiver.

She could hear it ringing on the other end of the line in the Sutton Place apartment. Marianne answered and reacted with great excitement. "It's your *daughter*. It's Robin!" Robin heard her shout, and then close up, her eager motherly voice. "How you been, honey? How's the weather in France?" at which point her mother cut in impatiently.

"Robin how *are* you? Everything all *right*?"

The tone was quavery, apprehensive. Robin said that everything was fine. She had seen the girl that morning.

"How *was* she?"

The surge of vitality in her mother's voice was thrilling yet pathetic. Carefully Robin chose her words. She said that the resemblance to her mother and Marya had been quite remarkable.

"Just *quite*?"

"More than quite. Very marked." She heard her mother's indrawn breath. She could picture her mother listening, sitting up in bed in pain, with her eyes desperately bright as she listened to Robin's description of that morning's breakfast, the girl's incredible beauty, and the father's overbearing behavior.

"But you didn't meet her face to face—or talk to her?"

"No, not yet . . ."

"Did you hear her voice?"

"No, she was at a distance . . . but Mother, please, don't jump to conclusions yet. Don't get your hopes up. Try to stay calm. It's too early to judge, and many obstacles lie ahead."

"Oh, I realize that, I realize that," said her mother tensely. "But this makes me so happy. This gives me so much hope. Oh, Robin, I'll be praying for you. Oh—wait a minute, please, try to get a picture of her, will you? If I see a picture I'll know for sure that she's my darling child."

When Robin hung up, she leaned against the phone booth, weak from emotion and the weight of responsibility. Never had she felt so alone, so in need of someone to help her. If only Andy hadn't had to go off to Hawaii, she could have called him and gotten his opinion on her next move. He could have suggested ways to contact the girl without enraging her tyrannical father . . . and made suggestions about the legal problems involved in such an unusual case.

But mostly she longed to hear his soothing voice reassuring her and guiding her—and telling her how much he loved her. It seemed an eon since she had lain in his arms and felt his warm, strong hand stroking her hair. He was so sensible, so intelligent, and yet so sympathetic.

But Andy wouldn't be back in the States for another two weeks. And she couldn't possibly wait for him. She needed advice—quickly—as to how to proceed, what the legal complications could be. So far she'd had only Madame Gautier to help her, but Madame Gautier was too excitable, too close to the situation to guide her. She should start looking for a lawyer, perhaps hire a detective to do some exhaustive research. But who and where in this city of utter strangers?

When she got back to the pension, Madame Voisin said she had a visitor.

"Who?" asked Robin. "And where is she?" She looked around the lobby, hoping to see Irène.

"It's a he," wheezed Madame Voisin with a knowing smirk and the droop of one eyelid. "Here's his card, *chérie*."

She drew it from her ample bosom and, feigning ignorance of its nature, handed it to Robin. On the slightly soiled bit of cardboard were the words M. RAOUL GUZMAN, AGENCE DE DÉTECTIVE PRIVÉ DE GUZMAN, 4 AVENUE MOLOTOFF, PARIS, FRANCE.

What a bit of luck. It seemed like the answer to a prayer.

He was strolling about the courtyard amid the pink geraniums—a broad-shouldered man of medium height, with kinky close-cropped graying hair, and a bushy moustache.

When he saw Madame Voisin beckoning to him, he came ambling in with a friendly smile.

"Mademoiselle Chodoff? Good morning." His brown eyes twinkled. "I'm Raoul Guzman, the fellow you talked to on the phone from New York. I was in the neighborhood this morning visiting my mother, and thought I'd drop by and say hello."

"How nice," she murmured.

"Don't mention it."

His voice was loud and emphatic and his French had a Parisian twang. Madame Voisin stood listening curiously, her hands clasped across her stomach and her piglike eyes darting back and forth.

"I was wondering if you'd care to have lunch with me, Mademoiselle Chodoff."

"How kind."

"I asked Madame Gautier to join us, but she can't make it. Too busy on a case. She thought maybe you'd like to talk to me about—certain matters—in private."

"Well, I would, monsieur. And thank you. I'll be right down."

As she ran up the winding staircase to change her clothes, she was conscious of his bold brown eyes upon her skimpy running shorts and bare muscular legs. But then, all Frenchmen, young and old, were prurient. She had learned that from her mother, who had had some Gallic beaux.

In her lamp-lit room, she peeled off her dank garments,

glad that she wouldn't have to eat lunch at the pension. Maybe Raoul Guzman could give her some authentic insight into Irène's background and real identity. Meanwhile, her sponge bath in the chilly water of the crockery pitcher proved most unsatisfactory, and again she wondered how anyone in the present century could put up with the accommodations Madame Voisin provided.

Clad in a loose white linen blouse and long yellow skirt, she descended the winding staircase to the lobby.

Guzman fingered his moustache, his eyes roving over her. *"Magnifique,"* he murmured, leading her by the elbow to the pension's front gate. From there they set off on foot for the Place du Vieux-Marché.

She had not yet visited the square where poor Joan of Arc had been burned alive. It proved to be a maelstrom of milling tourists, restaurants, souvenir shops, and cheap clothing stores, jammed into a long cobblestone alley (or narrow square) at the end of which there was a beautiful painted clock and a modern-istic church built in honor of St. Joan.

Threading their way past armies of German schoolboys and throngs of dazed old ladies following tour guides around, they finally reached their destination, a small nondescript res-taurant off the square. He said it had the best Normandy cooking in the city.

After the meager breakfast she had eaten, she was starved.

"I recommend the mussels with green sauce and an onion tart. They're super." He used the English word.

He also ordered two bottles of white wine, and as he drained his glass became more voluble about his profession and the clients he had worked for.

"Me? What do I do? Well, I can tell you, mademoiselle, that I love my work and am good at it, very good. I've been at it since I was in my teens. And my clients love me. They depend on me to track down information, and I track it down . . . to the bottom line."

"What kind of information do you track?" Robin asked, toying with her red-checked napkin.

"Adultery. Family matters. A boy from a good family wants to marry some chick he's met at a disco, and his mother and father want to know who she is, where she's from, has she slept around and contracted some disease, that sort of thing, and I never disappoint them. Or maybe some wife wants to find out her husband's secrets, how many mistresses he has, how often he sees them, and whether he's supporting a few bastards on the side."

"It sounds rather seamy."

"It's not all *that* seamy. I mean I also dig up information about wills, hunt for missing people, check on passports, and—"

"You hunt for missing people?" she interrupted.

"Oh sure. It's no big deal."

Their mussels and onion tarts arrived.

The food was delicious. Accompanying it was French bread, warm and smelling wonderful. She liked the mussels and the tasty green sauce, but found the onion tart a bit too rich.

Monsieur Guzman offered to finish it for her.

By then she had ventured to ask him whether he ever did investigative work in Rouen.

"But of course, mademoiselle. I was born in this city. I know it like the back of my hand, and almost all the people in it, except for the tourists, and they don't count." He laughed. His pitted face was flushed from all the wine he had consumed, and his voice had become louder, his diction a trifle slurred.

"May I ask you a question, monsieur?" Robin said. "I'm thinking of doing some research on a—certain family. And perhaps you'd be interested in helping. I'd pay you for your time."

"Well—naturally." He grinned. "I'd go out of business if I didn't charge fees. But maybe I'm not qualified to do the particular job. What's the name of the family?"

She hesitated, then she said, "D'Egremont. Do you know them?"

"Of course I know them. Not personally. But I've heard about them all my life. He's a bastard. And his wife's dead. I can tell you that right off the bat. So—what's your problem?"

Having cleaned his plate thoroughly with a chunk of bread, he took out a cigar and lit it.

"Well," Robin said, "I'm interested in knowing something about a certain daughter of the family. A young girl about twenty-two—Irène. I saw her this morning eating breakfast at the pension."

"Oh—Irène," he said. "Yes, she's a real doll." He puffed on his cigar, regarding her with his bloodshot eyes. "Of course you know that she's not his real child."

"Is that so?"

"Everybody knows it. You can guess it right away by the difference in their looks. Her mother was homely as sin and her father hasn't got one feature like hers. Look how tall he is, for instance, and how small-boned she is, and his nose is like a parrot's, whereas hers is pretty as a doll's."

Robin nodded.

He seemed very well informed.

"But is there any *real* proof that she's not his natural daughter?"

He shrugged. "I guess it's somewhere but I'd have to dig for it. It might cost you a bundle. OK?"

"How much?"

"Oh maybe a couple of hundred francs to start with." He looked her up and down. "But I wouldn't overcharge you. I'd make you a good price. What else would you like to know?"

"Well . . ." She felt a trifle panicky. She didn't particularly like him, or trust his boastful promises. "Well—what I'd mostly like to find out," she said, feeling her way along, "is something about her early life, where she was born, the date of her birth, and where she lived up to the age of four."

"Good enough. That sounds easy."

He reached into the inside pocket of his tweed jacket and produced a pad and a ballpoint pen. He scribbled a few words on the pad. "What else?"

"I'd like to talk to her alone if possible—if you can arrange it."

He raised his gray eyebrows and pursed his full wet lips. "That's a pretty big order."

"You mean she's never alone?"

"I don't know. I'll have to ask around." He dropped a cigar ash on his greasy dinner plate. "I don't know her personally."

"Where do they live?" Robin asked. "Do you happen to know?"

"Sure. In a cottage near the mouth of the Seine. The last plot of ground still left from his old estate."

"Then he *is* a real count?"

"Of course. From way back. And never lets anybody forget it." Guzman grinned.

"Then why would they come to a place like the Pension Bertrand for breakfast?"

He shrugged. "God knows. Probably because it's cheap. He's dead broke, I've heard. And it's also near the law courts, where he's got half a dozen suits pending. And is he addicted to lawsuits!" He belched and clapped his napkin to his mouth. "You better watch every move you make in his direction, or he'll slap a lawsuit on you and sue you for a million francs."

"But I'd like to drive out to his cottage," she said. "Perhaps meet her, if possible. Do you suppose I could rent a car and take a chance on finding her alone? Does he *ever* leave her by herself? Are there servants around? Or some nasty German shepherd?"

He shook his head.

"*Non*. Nothing of the sort." Smiling, he reached across the table and patted the back of her hand. "And you don't have to rent any car, baby. *I'm* here. *I* have a car. And I'll take you there for free."

"You *will*?"

"Why not? You hired me, didn't you? And I'm ready to start work—right now."

7

THRILLED BY HIS OFFER, she raced back to the pension to get her camera and returned, panting, to find him still eating his dessert—two apple pancakes on a large crockery platter.

"Sure you won't have some? They're the best in the city."

"No thank you, monsieur. I'm anxious to get started."

"Oh, the d'Egremonts will keep. They don't live much of a social life. If we don't catch them now we'll catch them another time."

His car was parked around the corner from the cul-de-sac. It was a cumbersome old black convertible with a soiled, ragged white top.

"It's a classic," he said, "but so big I couldn't get it up that damned alley of yours. But what an engine. They don't make them like this one anymore—*anywhere*—and I need something powerful in my work, in case I have to chase a suspect or make a quick getaway."

As she slid into the worn leather seat next to him, it struck her that the car must be known to many a criminal. People on the sidewalks were pausing to stare, and when he started the engine its roar mesmerized a whole busload of tourists.

Careening from the curb, they lurched wildly into the

traffic. He drove at top speed, cutting corners and jumping red lights, and the effect was made more jarring by the loud rock music he turned on. With the radio going full blast, they went roaring over the cobblestones, but mercifully soon reached the country, where the roads were narrower and harder to negotiate.

Rolling down her window and trying not to listen to the ersatz band and the out-of-date tunes pouring from the dashboard, she watched the passing villages, where copper pots were hung up for sale and small neat houses lined the quiet streets. They drove past acres of green farmland and apple orchards, meadows dotted with black-and-white cattle, and tall, tangled hedgerows separating the fields.

Brilliant red poppies grew wild along the roads. And far ahead stretched aisles of slender poplars just as she had seen them in many a French painting.

"Oh how lovely . . . how beautiful," she kept saying to herself as she breathed in the sweet odor of new-mown hay and freshly turned earth, and the wind blew her hair every which way in the sun.

At last, to her relief, he turned down the volume.

"Your first time in Normandy?" he asked in his husky voice.

"Yes," she replied.

"Weren't you here when your mother made that movie about the nun the Germans shot as a spy?"

"No, that was filmed in Hollywood," she said, "on a back lot at Twentieth Century."

"*Vraiment.* I can't believe it. I could have sworn it was made in Honfleur, a town not far from here."

The countryside grew more picturesque as they entered more primitive, winding roads, where small stone farmhouses and barns bigger than the houses stood surrounded by stone walls enclosing yards filled with chickens, ducks, and geese wandering in and out of muddy ponds with an incessant splashing.

Once they had to stop while a flock of sheep crossed the road in the care of a boy in a blue smock, and once a troop of rosy-cheeked children in uniforms and carrying schoolbags stood gawking at the car from the side of the road.

"This is the real Normandy," Guzman said with a touch of pride, "but most of it's been rebuilt since World War Two."

"It looks as though it had always been here."

"Well, it hasn't. The damned Allies turned most of it to rubble."

The road kept winding, and the villages fell away. He turned left up a dirt lane, and they jounced through deep woods at a snail's pace for a couple of miles. From time to time she caught glimpses of blue water, and then they rounded a curve, and the woods ended in a broad, overgrown meadow, with a view of blue sea at its far end.

"That's the Channel," he said, pointing toward the sparkling water. Turning off the radio, he gazed around quickly and slowed the car, almost to a crawl. "All this property used to belong to the d'Egremont family. Over there"—he pointed toward a few straggly trees not far from the water—"was their château. During the war it was taken over by the Germans as a headquarters for their Luftwaffe officers, and then the Allies came along and bombed it to bits."

She stared at the poor-looking trees as they bounced slowly over the deeply rutted meadow. "Was it a big château?" she asked.

"God yes. And gorgeous. Very old. Built in the twelfth century. The original part, that is. Then some eighteenth-century ancestor did it over and added wings and staircases and gardens in the Louis Quatorze style. They say that in the cellars there were dungeons and tunnels to the sea. But it's gone now. And he's never gotten over it. He lives to rebuild it."

She had spied a small stone cottage at the very edge of the sea.

"Is that where they live now?"

"Right. That's the place."

It looked barely bigger than a fisherman's hut. Even from a distance it looked so forlorn and dilapidated that one might have thought it abandoned.

"Pretty nothing, eh?" grinned Guzman. "But that's all he has left, that shack and half an acre. They say he'd do anything to get the rest of it back. Even sell his daughter."

"Are you kidding?"

"Listen." He frowned. "In France a man's land is his proudest possession. It means more to him than his wife, his kids, even his mistress. It's his life, his ego."

"Has he tried to sell his daughter?"

Guzman shrugged. He stopped the car and turned off the engine. "People say he takes her up to Deauville to meet millionaires who come there to gamble. They say he's dickering with some drug mogul from the island of Martinique that he met at the casino who wants to marry her."

"My God!" Robin's heart sank as she remembered Madame Gautier's words over the phone to her mother about the "emergency situation," and the father and daughter's plans to leave for Martinique "in about a week."

"As I said," Guzman continued as he reached over and opened the door of the convertible on her side, "he's a first-class son of a bitch, and obsessed, so look out for him."

"Aren't you coming with me?"

"I thought you wanted to talk to her *alone*." He looked at her blandly.

"Well—I do—of course—but . . ."

"Look, I know you can handle it," he said, "and you'll do much better without me." Reaching into the pocket of his jacket, he produced a police whistle. "I'll be right back there in those woods watching everything that happens, and if you need me, just blow this." He handed her the whistle.

"How far back in the woods?"

"Listen, I'd only ruin it. He'd *know* you were up to something."

For a long moment she stared at him steadily and coldly. Then she slid from the car and began running toward the cottage. As she ran, she could hear the sound of his motor starting, and the radio beginning to blast.

* * *

The music faded behind her, and then there was only the sound of her feet rustling through tall weeds.

The closer she came to the cottage, the more deserted it appeared.

Even at a distance she could see that two of the windows were broken. A wooden door sagged half-open on its hinges. Coming up to the rough stone walls, she peered through one of the broken panes and glimpsed a crude stone floor on which stood a rusty iron bedstead half covered with a ragged quilt. Next to the bed was a bushel basket heaped with shells.

She walked twice around the small building. There was no path to its front door and the front door wobbled ominously when she pushed it open. The place stank of fish and mildew. Lobster pots and fishing gear leaned against a wall.

They couldn't be *living* here full time.

Frowning, she walked slowly to the edge of the cliff. She looked down its sandy sides spotted with underbrush and could see the Normandy coastline stretching away on either side in a splendid panorama of scalloped green bluffs rising from narrow graveled beaches. The water was calm, the sky clear, the sun bright. It was hard to believe that this serene landscape had once been the scene of battle, with planes roaring overhead, fire bursting from the cliffs, and men climbing to their deaths up steep sandy slopes.

She heard a soft voice behind her.

The girl was standing a few feet away. "*Excusez-moi,*" she was saying shyly, "are you looking for the battlefield?"

Irène d'Egremont had changed since breakfast to a faded blue cotton skirt and peasant blouse. Her feet were bare and her long hair tangled. She was carrying a fishing rod and a wooden bucket.

"No," Robin said. "I was looking for you."

As though she hadn't heard, the girl gestured down the coast. "If you are looking for the Omaha Beach where the Americans came, it is down that way."

"Thank you," Robin said, "but I came to see *you*. My name is Robin Chodoff." She held out her hand. "I saw you this morning at the Pension Bertrand, and I thought you looked so much like my younger sister. She disappeared eighteen years ago—in Central Park."

The girl nodded vaguely. She showed little interest.

"Her name was Marya," Robin said, trying to look into Irène's brown eyes. "She was four years old when it happened, and we've been searching for her ever since."

"Oh . . . I'm sorry . . ."

Her voice was sweet and musical, but it revealed no trace of emotion. She was merely being polite. "What a pity." She began edging toward the cottage.

"Oh please don't go," said Robin. "I came all the way from New York to see you." The girl kept moving. "Have you ever been to New York?"

"*Non, mademoiselle.*"

"It's a big big city, much bigger than Rouen. And there's a park in the middle with a seal pool and a zoo."

The girl smiled fleetingly. She glanced toward the woods.

"That's where she disappeared, in that park, on her way to the zoo. Somebody snatched her." She looked intensely into the girl's eyes.

"*Vraiment?*"

But the response was uninterested, in fact obviously distracted. "Will you excuse me?" She moved more quickly toward the fisherman's hut. "I must cook the dinner." She glanced into her bucket, where Robin could glimpse a small fish swimming about.

"I'm sorry. I didn't mean to keep you. I wonder if we could get together sometime for a little talk."

Irène raised her beautiful brown eyes as though in panic.

"*Non* . . . I'm sorry," she stammered, with the color flooding into her beautiful face. "I am going away soon. And tomorrow I—have an appointment—with someone . . ."

"OK, well then will you call me when you return from

your appointment tomorrow? At the Pension Bertrand? That's where I'm staying. Or you could just ask for me when you come there for breakfast. The name is Robin Chodoff."

"Chodoff . . ."

Vaguely she nodded.

She had reached the front door of the cottage at last, and in her haste she kicked it open frantically with her bare foot. Her behavior reminded Robin of a caged bird that has lived so long behind the steel bars of its cage, it is frightened to emerge when the door is open. All it wants to do is remain in its prison.

Even so, once inside the security of the hut, she remembered her manners.

"*Au revoir, mademoiselle.*" She summoned a shy smile. "It was very nice to meet you."

"It's wonderful to meet *you*," Robin said with feeling.

"*Merci* . . ."

She turned her back and was about to close the door when Robin remembered her mother's request.

"Oh—may I take your picture, please?"

"My *picture*?" She cringed back behind the wooden door.

"It will only take a minute or two," Robin said, marching into the dilapidated, dim room. "Please. You're so pretty. And it's such a beautiful view."

"But I'm not dressed. I look terrible."

"You look lovely. Please, mademoiselle, I'm sure that anyone in America who sees your picture will fall in love with you."

"Oh—never." With a deprecatory little laugh Irène took a step forward into the sunlight streaming through the half-open door. "They will laugh at me."

"Not a bit. They'll think you're the reincarnation of a famous movie star."

At last, thanks to these blandishments, she succeeded in getting Irène out of the hut. And it was encouraging to see that she possessed a touch of vanity. For, smoothing down her hair, and stuffing her blouse into her skirt, she actually posed for the camera and assumed a fetching smile. And it was going to be a beautiful shot—with the shadows of the hut giving depth to the background and the afternoon sun shimmering on the masses of hair, the sweet girlish face.

Robin pressed the shutter.

Simultaneously she heard the sound of a shot.

The girl froze, as though the bullet had hit her. Then, with a cry, she fled into the hut and slammed the door behind her.

Wheeling around, Robin saw the count standing a few yards away.

Dressed in hunting jacket and tweed hat, he bore a smoking shotgun. Slung over his shoulder from a leather strap hung a brace of dead rabbits, dripping blood from their limp paws.

"What are you doing here? This is private property!" he bellowed.

His face was beet-red and his walk uncertain.

Summoning an innocent smile, she answered, "I didn't realize, monsieur. I was looking for the battle site."

"No battles were fought here," he announced pompously. "Can't you read? This is private property. The signs are everywhere."

"I didn't see them," she said. And, indeed, she had not. There were only the woods, the wide meadow, and the sea. "I'm very sorry." She started walking toward the woods.

"Just a minute, young lady."

He strode after her, with his bloody rabbits bouncing against his leather boots. She stopped walking and he came abreast of her and stood again in her path. She could smell the fumes of alcohol on his breath. "Let me see that camera."

"Why? It's mine."

"Hand it over, please."

"No, monsieur!"

She put the camera behind her back and gazed at him defiantly. She thought of blowing her whistle, but decided against it.

"Hand it over," he barked.

"The hell with you." She glared at him.

"GIVE IT TO ME—*bitch!*"

She zigzagged away, clutching the camera to her breast. The going was hard over the ancient cow meadow. There were ruts, waist-high weeds, and holes into which she stumbled.

"*Arrêtez!*" she heard him shout. "*Arrêtez ou je tire!*"

Reaching into her pocket for Guzman's whistle, she blew a shrill blast.

At the same instant a shot rang out.

The bullet whizzed over her right shoulder. She threw herself down in the waist-high grass.

Again he fired, before she could rise and race for the woods. The bullet whined above her head. And then he was upon her and jerking her to her feet. Almost purple with anger, he pulled the camera strap from around her neck, and then, as she fought to snatch the camera from his hands, threw it on the ground and stamped on it again and again until it fell to pieces.

"You filthy bastard," she breathed.

Paying no attention, he stooped and picked up the ruined roll of film. Stuffing it into his jacket, he strode off toward the stone cottage by the sea.

When she reached the woods, Guzman and the car were gone.

8

SHE WALKED SLOWLY over dead leaves under the shadow of flickering tree branches. Gradually her breathing quieted, and the fury and contempt she felt for d'Egremont, and to a lesser extent for Guzman, began to die down to feelings of dull resentment and puzzlement. In some ways the adventure had been her own fault. She should never have gone off with a stranger on so harebrained a safari. But on the other hand how could she have predicted the sheer insanity of d'Egremont? He was a psychopath, a murderer who deserved to be locked up.

Meanwhile, she was miles from Rouen. Even when she emerged from the woods onto a narrow macadam highway, she was still out in the country with no houses in sight.

Trudging along in the hot sunlight in her crumpled linen outfit, she at last came upon a peaceful little settlement with walled farmhouses and a church—but no phone booths, and no people anywhere in sight.

No buses came by. Occasionally a car passed, but none stopped or even slowed down on the seemingly endless, winding country roads.

Finally, in one of the small villages, she saw a woman hanging up clothes behind a little stone house covered with red roses, and she asked her where she could find a telephone.

The woman said that she was welcome to use hers in the kitchen. When Robin asked the number of the nearest cab company, she smiled and said that her daughter, Jeanette, who was due home from school at six o'clock, would be happy to drive her back to Rouen.

"Just make yourself comfortable, mademoiselle. Would you like a glass of water? Some cider, perhaps?"

"No thank you, madame. How kind of you."

Robin sat in the dark, cool parlor, studying the sacred pictures on the walls and the small candlelit shrine in a corner.

The woman was baking bread. When she had put her loaves into the oven she came in and said that her old mother, who was blind, would love to meet her. "Her room is upstairs," she said. "All day she sits in the window facing the road, listening for the people going by. Sometimes they call to her and some stop in to visit her, which she likes very much. She keeps herself amused by thinking about their lives."

She led the way up winding stone steps, and they entered a small room with a single window at the far end. In the patch of sunlight cast by the window, an old woman in a close-fitting linen cap sat on a wooden rocker. As Robin entered, she turned her clouded eyes toward her, and her small wrinkled face lit up with expectancy.

"*Bonjour, mademoiselle.*" Her voice was soft, tremulous, and fluty. "*Asseyez-vous, s'il vous plaît.*" When Robin sat down next to her, she reached for Robin's hand and held it against her cheek. Her skin was dry and papery. She was a hundred years old, her daughter said.

But her mind was clear and her memory keen. In her quaint-sounding French she asked Robin about America. She liked Americans. "Twice they came here and helped us. And one of them still writes us. He came here too, last year with his grandchildren." She spoke of the war, when they had lived in the cellars. "There was nothing left in the village and every morning at dawn we crept out and saw the dead soldiers lying everywhere." She had known the martyred nun whom Robin's mother had played on film. "Ah, she was a saint—hiding people and bringing them food. And your mother, she must be a very good woman to act her part, and I wish that I could see her but I'm sure it would make me cry."

Gradually, as Robin sat there in the fading luminous light, the rage she had felt against d'Egremont began to dissipate.

Soon she found herself telling the old woman about her lost sister and her mother's great grief and hope of someday finding her. And the filmed eyes watched her. Robin saw tears trickling down the withered cheeks. Gently the old woman kept patting her hand and nodding. "*Eh bien,*" she said at last, "you will find her, never fear. God will somehow work a miracle, if you trust Him and have faith." The dying light of the afternoon rested on her shriveled face and for a moment the dead eyes seemed to glow with a strange beauty.

Deeply moved, Robin bent and kissed her, and the old woman turned and kissed her in return. Her kiss was light and dry as an autumn leaf, and when Robin patted her, she whispered, "I will pray for you." Then she made the sign of the cross.

"Mademoiselle, my daughter is here." From below, the lady of the house was calling her. As Robin tiptoed down the stone steps, she felt great peace.

9

THE WOMAN'S DAUGHTER, Jeanette, was just as friendly and pleasant as the rest of the family. Even though she had worked all day as a teacher and had supper to cook for her invalid husband, she drove Robin all the way to the pension in her pickup truck. When they parted, they promised to write to one another.

"*Au revoir. Merci mille fois . . .*" As Robin stood waving to the truck backing down the cul-de-sac, she heard a frenzied voice from the shadows behind her.

"*Mon Dieu, chérie*. Where have you been?" croaked Madame Gautier, running out of the tunnel entrance. "I've been waiting for hours. Madame Voisin said you'd gone to lunch with Raoul Guzman, but I expected you back long ago. Where *were* you?"

She gasped and narrowed her eyes when Robin told her that Guzman had taken her to the d'Egremont cottage. "But how crazy of him. What right had he interfering in my plans?"

"He offered to take me. I was going to rent a car," Robin began, but Madame Gautier whisked Robin up to her lamp-lit room and, perching tensely on the edge of the sleigh bed, began firing questions at her. Every detail of Robin's trip to the cottage seemed to upset her violently. When Robin told her that d'Egremont had shot at her and smashed her camera, her face contorted, her nostrils flared, and she looked about to faint. Closing her eyes and clinging to the head of the sleigh bed, she shivered as though the room were icy cold.

"*Mon Dieu.* He might have killed you. And where was Raoul all this time?"

"In the car . . . back in the woods . . . listening to music."

"In the *woods*? Listening to *music!*" Madame Gautier smote her forehead. "Why did he not accompany you?"

"He said I could handle it better alone."

"Bah! But when d'Egremont attacked you, did he accost that wicked creature?"

"No."

"What happened?"

"He disappeared."

"*Disappeared.* Oh, the coward . . . the—the crocodile!" Madame Gautier rose. Still trembling, she choked out, "It's too much. I'm going to call him and tell him our friendship is over. He is never to come near us or interfere with my arrangements ever again . . . or—or the things I've planned for us."

She stormed from the room and headed for the winding staircase.

Puzzled and disturbed by this overwrought reaction, Robin followed. "Please, Madame Gautier. I asked him to help me. I shouldn't have gone with him."

"Nonsense." Madame Gautier turned. "He never should have taken you there. It wasn't his place."

She vanished down the staircase.

From below, from the concierge's office where the house phone was, her angry voice could be heard berating the invisible Guzman. A long pause ensued, then mutterings and deep silences. When she came back upstairs her face was fiery and her eyes had a haunted look. Sweat was pouring down her rouged cheeks in red rivulets. Robin had never seen her so upset.

Perching uneasily on the bed again, Madame Gautier lit a cigarette with a shaking hand, and then turned her close-set eyes on Robin in a long, melancholy stare.

"I'm sorry to have made such a spectacle of myself, *chérie*, but the events of this afternoon have deeply disturbed me." She wiped her moist forehead with the back of her hand. "I had *so* looked forward to telling you about tomorrow, but now it's all been spoiled."

"What's happening tomorrow?" Robin asked, trying to placate her.

Madame Gautier shook her head mournfully and drew deeply on her cigarette.

"What were you going to tell me, madame?"

"A—most wonderful scheme . . . to see her in private."

"Irène?"

"*Oui.*" Her voice sounded flat. Again she fell silent. Her gaze moved to the oil paintings and then rested on her lap.

"What had you planned, madame?"

Madame Gautier heaved a heavy sigh. "Ah, it took so much trouble and split-second timing." She walked over to the cupboard and took out the bottle of wine. Pulling out two glasses, she slopped wine into them both. "Tomorrow, most fortuitously, Irène's prospective fiancé from Martinique is arriving in Caen by train from Paris. And d'Egremont is meeting him at the railroad station at one. *Without* Irène. She'll be alone for possibly an hour."

"So we can *really* talk."

Madame Gautier brightened slightly. "If it all works out as I've planned it," she said, bringing the wineglasses to the side of the bed. "I've reserved a suite for us at the Caen hotel. We can go up there early and wait for him to leave. Then you'll sneak into her room and have a good long chat."

"Wonderful," said Robin. "Although I didn't find her too responsive today. She didn't seem interested in what I had to say."

"Maybe because her father was around," Madame Gautier said. "The circumstances were wrong. She didn't dare relax with you."

"And you think she might relax tomorrow—with her fiancé expected?"

Madame Gautier's face crumpled. "Oh please, please don't put *more* obstacles in the way, *chérie*. Be hopeful. Be confident. You'll have at least an hour with her and you're a very intelligent person . . . very sympathetic, resourceful . . . I *know* you'll think of a way to break her down."

"I'll try."

Feeling sorry about Madame Gautier's bleak expression, Robin added, "She does seem quite docile, and she's very polite."

"Do you think she's your sister?"

Standing up, holding her glass, Madame Gautier's eyes looked desperately into Robin's.

"I'm not sure—yet, madame."

"But—but you think she *might* be . . . ?"

"She might," Robin said.

"Oh thank God . . . oh Holy Mother of God!" Laying aside her cigarette and wineglass, Madame Gautier took Robin in her arms. She was shivering as though with cold. Her tears fell on Robin's neck.

In the empty dining room next morning, they ate breakfast at six o'clock. The chairs were still piled on the bare wooden tables. Madame Sophie, in her pink plastic curlers, glumly served them lukewarm coffee and stale rolls.

It was raining when they emerged from the Pension Bertrand. As they peered down the cul-de-sac toward the street beyond, not a cab was to be seen at that hour of the morning in that desolate part of town.

Madame Gautier was wearing her long nurse's cape, but had no umbrella, only a flimsy plastic rain scarf tied under her chin.

And Robin had brought along only the skimpiest of collapsible umbrellas, the kind that are easy to tuck into a purse or a duffel bag, but are of very little use in a cold driving storm sweeping in from the Channel.

As they were standing there under the dripping, cavelike entrance, a thin piping voice sounded in their ears. It was Jean-Pierre, Sophie's starved-looking little son, carrying a big, cotton man-size black umbrella. "Don't worry, *mesdames*. I find you the taxi." Off he scampered into the rain, dragging the umbrella, then belatedly struggling to put it up against the wind, which he somehow succeeded in doing before Robin could reach him and help.

"Poor child." She turned to Madame Gautier after watching him scurry away with the umbrella over the slippery cobblestones like a mushroom with legs. "He's going to be soaked."

"Oh, he's a tough little bird," said Madame Gautier. "I wouldn't worry about him."

"But he does so much work, and they take such advantage."

Madame Gautier shrugged. "In France we don't believe in pampering children."

"How old is he?"

"I have no idea. I was away when he was born. In fact I don't even know which one of the guests his father was . . ."

"The *guests*?"

"Here he comes now."

Somehow Jean-Pierre had found them a cab, and he was riding precariously on the running board as it came jolting up over the cobblestones. Robin reached into her pocketbook and handed him ten francs. But he shook his head with the beautiful blue eyes wide, and said politely, "*Merci, mademoiselle*. It is not permitted."

"All right then. I'll bring you back a present from Caen."

"Shh," said Madame Gautier, obviously alarmed that Robin had betrayed their destination.

Robin ignored her. The cab engine kept running. "How about a spaceship? Do you have a spaceship?"

"*Non, mademoiselle.*"

"Then I'll bring you one. OK?"

"*Mais oui.*" He grinned shyly. His meekness and hopefulness broke her heart. "*Merci beaucoup, mademoiselle.*"

Robin patted his soft blond hair. He looked up at her trustingly, and again she felt her heart melt with sadness and the desire to do something nice for him. "*Vite, vite!*" Madame Gautier called from the cab. "*Viens donc!* Or we'll miss our train."

They arrived at the station two hours early, and had to sit reading newspapers and watching the commuters leave for Paris or points north.

Madame Gautier spent most of the time in the ladies' room. "It's my nerves," she explained. "Whenever I'm excited, my insides go to pieces. Even on my wedding day I could scarcely get up the aisle and all I could think of was that the ceremony would be short so I could run to the WC."

The train to Caen was crowded. They couldn't get seats together. Madame Gautier sat far ahead and Robin could see her stirring restlessly and looking around desperately as though seeking a restroom. But as the train slowed down for its stop at Caen, she turned around and smiled in Robin's direction, raising her hand and making the "V for Victory" sign.

The rain kept falling. It was hard to find a taxi. They drove through drab streets, past cathedrals and scaffolded buildings shrouded in mist, and finally drew up to the curb on a sordid commercial street, where, sandwiched between a boarded-up movie house and a horse-meat shop, was a large decaying hotel in the *fin-de-siècle* style.

"*Mon Dieu,*" said Madame Gautier, eyeing its stained facade and crumbling stone balconies. "It used to be so stylish. The prince of Parma stayed here."

Robin stood under the broken-glass marquee while Madame Gautier paid the driver. "Hôtel de la Reine Matilde." She could barely make out the lettering.

"I just can't believe it," said Madame Gautier as they

climbed the filthy steps to a smeary glass door, above which was a neon sign bearing the legend BIÈRE, VIN BLANC, VIN ROUGE, SANDWICH, CHAMBRES LIBRES.

The lobby was high-ceilinged with marble pillars that must once have been splendid. Madame Gautier had to rush off to the ladies' room, so Robin registered and was given a huge brass key for Suite 617. Sweeping up from the lobby was a broad flight of marble stairs covered with dingy red carpeting, and next to it an old-fashioned elevator of iron and glass in which the passengers resembled larvae inside a chrysalis.

Slowly the car shuddered up through the open atrium of the building as though it were about to break down at any moment. With a jolt it came to rest in a cavernous gallery of few light bulbs and many large doors.

Deep silence prevailed. No maids were in sight. *"Mon Dieu!"* Madame Gautier kept saying. "It used to be the height of elegance. The best people came here."

Suite 617 had huge double doors. The knob of one was missing. When Madame Gautier inserted the immense key in the lock, it refused to budge, and not until they'd both tried several times did the door creak open.

Madame Gautier meanwhile had kept turning her head toward the doors opposite. "I wonder if they've come yet," she whispered. "I wonder if they're in there. I don't want them to hear us."

The suite they had been given was large and gloomy, full of dusty furniture. A single light bulb hanging from the ceiling illumined the dismal salon. In the high-ceilinged bedroom, unmade beds with stained mattresses and a dresser adorned with rolls of toilet paper lay awaiting their pleasure. A roach scuttled across Robin's hand when she turned on the torn pink-chiffon lamp. Rust rimmed the ancient bathtub and sink, and the toilet had not been flushed.

"Quelle horreur!" Madame Gautier recoiled, throwing up her hands. "What a nerve. Who would stay here? He must be crazy."

"Shall I go back down and try to change it?"

"*Non*. We'll only be here for a couple of hours . . . and I asked for a suite across the hall from theirs."

The salon overlooked a small parking lot, and behind the drawn green shade Madame Gautier perched on the arm of an upholstered chair to await the arrival of the count's brown limousine.

She described the car to Robin. "It's very old with patches of rust and the stuffing is out of the seat cushions. He really is poor. I don't know how he exists."

The minutes passed.

Robin wished she'd brought a magazine.

She wanted to run downstairs to the busy commercial street and see if she could find a toy shop, but Madame Gautier wouldn't hear of it.

"We can do all that later. This is what we came for. Let's not miss our opportunity."

At twelve-fifteen she uttered a hoarse shriek.

"Look. Come quickly . . . but keep out of sight."

Robin peeked from behind the shade and beheld the count, in a raincoat and with a black umbrella, climbing from the front seat of a very ancient Lincoln. He slammed the door and circled around the back of the car to help his daughter from the passenger seat.

Robin could see only her legs, slim and shapely in black silk stockings and high-heeled black pumps, before she was swallowed up under her father's umbrella. Arm in arm, the two walked across the rainy parking lot toward the hotel.

On tiptoe Madame Gautier moved to the door of the suite. She opened it an inch and peered out into the hall.

Their suite wasn't far from the elevator. In a few minutes they could hear the groaning and creaking of the old glass cage ascending the shaft.

"Here they come," whispered Madame Gautier with her eyes intensely bright.

The elevator car stopped with its cargo of black larvae.

Amid clatter and clanking and a muttered exclamation or two the count and Irène finally emerged. As they passed Suite 617 Irène looked strangely elegant in her long black coat with a black lace mantilla draped over her hair, which she wore in a *chignon*. Small jet earrings glittered at her ears and the high-heeled shoes gave her walk grace and dignity . . . even a certain measure of sexiness. But her expression was still melancholy. The beautiful dark eyes were downcast and dejected under the pointed eyebrows. She reminded Robin of a young Spanish widow on her way to her husband's funeral.

Their suite was across the hall a few doors down from 617.

Robin could hear the count inserting his key into the lock and experiencing the same difficulties they had with theirs.

"*Diable!*" she heard him mutter and then more rattling sounds. Robin started giggling but Madame Gautier, horrified, put her finger to her lips. They heard him saying to Irène, "Now, Irène, I want to make sure you know how to open this door when the time comes. Because when I get back with Monsieur Quintana there'll be no one but you to let us in."

"*Oui, Papa.*"

"*Bon.* Let's go in and you can try it."

The door banged. In another few seconds muffled clicking noises could be heard and then the sound of his voice expostulating from inside.

"*Non. Non! Très mauvais.* Turn it *slowly*—to the *right!*"

"I'm sorry, Papa." Thinly they could hear her apology from within.

The door opened and he emerged. "Now stay right here and don't let anybody in. I'll be back in an hour with your fiancé, so please be ready and see that everything is prepared. The wine chilled . . . and the meat sliced."

"*Oui, Papa.*"

He closed the door, waited to hear the key turn in the lock, and then strutted past Suite 617, a red-faced, evil-humored brute with a military bearing. Robin watched him with hatred as he rang for the elevator and tapped his foot when it did not come immediately. Every movement was impatient, irascible, and belligerent, as though he were not only waging a war with humanity but taking his frustrations out on every inanimate object in his path.

As the car removed him from view, Madame Gautier stepped back from their door with eyes glittering.

"Oh, Robin, *chérie*." She slid her arm around Robin's waist. "From now on, it's up to you."

"And *her*," said Robin gravely.

"*Non . . . non . . .* it's your decision." Her voice caught in her throat in an odd, strangulated sort of way. "So please be honest with yourself. Be *honest!*" she said, with a strange look in her eyes. Then she leaned forward and kissed Robin, a fierce kiss on the mouth.

"God bless you, *ma petite*."

Sliding her arm from Robin's waist, she pushed her gently into the corridor. The door of Suite 617 closed.

10

MYSTIFIED AND DEEPLY confused by Madame Gautier's behavior, Robin stood irresolute for several seconds, then, taking a deep breath, crossed the hall and knocked on the door of the d'Egremont suite.

She heard the sound of water running.

She knocked again. The water was turned off with a clamor of pipes.

"Mademoiselle d'Egremont . . . ?" she called, with her lips close to the door.

There was silence, then quick footsteps. "Who is it?" the girl asked.

"The maid, mademoiselle."

"*Un moment, s'il vous plaît.*"

She heard the girl struggling with the lock, then the door opened on Irène d'Egremont. She wore a white terry-cloth robe and her hair, damp and curly, was tumbled on her shoulders.

"*Pardon.* I was showering," she began, and then broke off, with widening eyes. "But you're not the maid, you're the girl who came to see us yesterday."

She started to close the door. "I'm sorry—I can't let you in."

"Please!" Robin said, pushing against the door with her

shoulder. "I have to talk to you—while your father is out. It's important. An emergency. It's your life. It could save your life." She shoved the door back wide.

The girl had backed away into a large dim room with a crystal chandelier and tall chairs set around a table. Her face was pale.

"I don't understand," she gasped. "What do you mean— save my life?"

"I didn't mean to upset you. I just need to ask you some questions."

"About *what*?"

Clutching her robe, she glided around to the other side of the lace-covered table. It was set with dishes, wine bottles, glasses—no doubt ordered in advance from the hotel management for the arrival of Monsieur Quintana of Martinique.

"Can we sit down for a few minutes?" Robin asked. "I have some pictures I'd like to show you, but they won't take long and I promise to be gone long before your father gets back."

"I'm afraid I haven't the time. As you can see we're expecting a guest."

"This won't take more than a few minutes." Quickly Robin produced a manila envelope and began drawing out photos. She spread them on the table. "Please do me a favor. Just look at them—please—*please!*" The girl's startled brown eyes met hers across the table, and then she came around the lace tablecloth and stood at Robin's side.

"Do you recognize this man?"

It was a portrait of Leopold Chodoff, taken when he was young and just starting his career. With arms folded, he stared at the camera, his gray eyes intent and his black hair slicked down.

Irène picked up the picture. She stared at it, frowning.

"Ever seen him before?"

"No," Irène replied. She laid it down. "Who is he?"

"My father," Robin replied. She looked up at Irène. "And perhaps yours."

"*Mine?*" The girl gave a little laugh. "What do you mean? I *have* a father."

Robin did not reply. She reached for another picture. "Do you remember this woman?"

It was a snapshot of her mother taken nineteen years before, in Hollywood, in front of a Spanish-style house. Marya had been three years old. Her mother was holding her by the hand and smiling at the camera. She looked very slim and radiant. Marya's hair was cut short in bangs and she was wearing a gingham sunsuit.

"She's beautiful," said Irène, looking down at the photograph. "And so is the little girl. Is she her daughter?"

"Yes."

"They look so much alike."

"They look like you too, *n'est-ce pas?*" asked Robin, again looking up into her face.

"Oh no . . . they're much prettier."

Robin put the two pictures back into the envelope and fished for another. The girl touched her shoulder.

"Mademoiselle, may I ask why you are showing me these things? What have they to do with *my* life?"

"I'd hoped you might recognize some of the people in them," Robin answered. "But you haven't, have you? *Honestly?*" Once again she tried to gaze into the beautiful brown eyes.

"*Non*, I'm afraid they mean nothing to me. Who are they?"

"My parents, and my little sister, who was kidnapped eighteen years ago."

"*Oh. Comme c'est tragique.*"

She looked sympathetic, rather like someone at a funeral politely paying tribute to the family of the deceased.

But as Robin kept searching her face for some more heartfelt reaction, she lowered her eyes and plucked nervously at her robe. In a faltering tone, she asked, "May I see the rest of them?"

"Certainly," said Robin.

Quickly she took out the last two photographs in the small collection she had brought from home. Her family had never been ones for taking pictures. When she'd searched the house, she had found no albums and only a handful of prints scattered in her mother's desk drawer.

One of these was a small faded snapshot of herself and Marya roller-skating in front of the Fifty-seventh Street apartment. The old white-haired doorman was in the background. And the other was a big eight-by-ten glossy taken by a professional photographer in Central Park a few days before their father left home.

Irène d'Egremont picked up the glossy.

It showed two children seated astride a couple of Central Park ponies. Both girls were dressed in elaborate cowboy costumes and both looked miserable, particularly Marya, whose round baby face, with its somber brown eyes under the big cowboy sombrero, seemed a symbol of the unhappiness to come.

The girl stared at it in silence.

"This is you?" she asked, pointing to the older of the two girls on horseback.

"*Oui.*"

"And the little one?"

"My sister. The one who was kidnapped."

"Ah. She's so sad-looking!"

"Yes. Do you know why?"

"*Non.* Why?"

"Because she was afraid our father was going to leave us. She sensed that that was why he'd bought us those cowboy outfits and taken us for a pony ride." Her voice caught as the memory of that autumn afternoon swept over her, the vivid recollection of her father's false joviality as he'd bustled about, lifting them on and off the horses, and telling them to smile for the birdie and he'd buy them an ice cream cone.

"Ah, *pauvres petites,*" the girl said, still studying the picture. "Was it another woman?"

"No," Robin said. "Not as far as I know."

"Then why would he leave those two beautiful children?"

"For pride maybe. You see my mother is a very famous actress. She was on television. And my father was just a poor struggling musician at that time."

"*Oh—je comprends.*"

"Later he became famous. He conducted a lot in Europe. Leopold Chodoff. Ever heard of him?"

"No, I'm afraid not," she said, reddening. "You see I go very few places. I love music and the movies, but Papa does not approve. But I envy you with two such gifted and handsome parents."

"They could be *your* parents," Robin said impulsively.

"*My* parents?" The pointed eyebrows went up.

Robin moved toward her quickly. She tried to take her hand. "I think that there's a real possibility they might be," she said. "I think that if you look deep, *deep* into your heart, you might find them both still there."

"Oh, I don't understand you, mademoiselle."

She drew away, flustered, her hand on her breast—toward the tall, uncurtained windows, where the rain kept beating against the glass.

"Please try to remember the time you were very small," Robin said in a low, intense voice. "Try to look back on—on scenes from the past . . . images . . . and objects. A bedroom with lambs frisking over the wallpaper . . . a gold locket in the shape of a heart . . . and a big building, an apartment house with an elevator . . . a dollhouse with a doll family that Mother changed while we were asleep . . . and Daddy in the mirror, waving a stick while the music played." Tears choked her words. "And—and the turtles Uncle Harry bought us on Valentine's Day."

The girl kept staring at her blankly. It was impossible to read her thoughts. And the rain slashed against the panes.

"You cried when they died," Robin said softly.

"*Who* died?"

"The turtles . . . Benny and Sam."

As Robin spoke, the girl's eyes lit up with a strange brightness. "B-B Benny and S-Sam . . . !" she breathed.

Robin nodded. She held her breath. In that moment she felt as though she were on the brink of discovery. She was standing on the edge of a sea, watching a ship slowly rising from the deeps where it had lain long hidden. In another moment it would appear, intact and miraculous . . .

As they gazed at one another in the rain-darkened room and time seemed to stand still, the phone rang.

Robin started, and the girl's head turned instantly toward the sound. As though galvanized, her body quivered, and then she ran toward a door at the end of the salon. "*Excusez-moi,*" she breathed. Pulling the door open, she disappeared into a dark hallway, closing the door behind her.

Robin stood on trembling legs, still dazed, but deeply infuriated. What a time for the phone to ring, and what an effort it might be to restore the magic spell it had taken such pains to build. She stood there breathing rapidly, and then began pacing the worn carpet of the huge salon. Five minutes went by, then ten. Fifteen minutes passed. If the phone call didn't end soon, there would be no time left before the count was due to return.

She was just gathering up her photographs when she heard footsteps and Irène hurried in.

Her hair was up and she was dressed once more in the long black coat, high heels, and black stockings.

"I'm sorry, mademoiselle," she faltered, avoiding Robin's eyes. "But I must leave immediately. My father has just called from the train station and he wants me to meet him there at once."

"Oh dear," said Robin. "We were just getting started. When can I see you again?"

"I-I'm not sure. I-I'll be very busy for the next few days . . . I'll try to call you." She had headed for the door and was sticking the big key into the lock.

"I'll be at the Pension Bertrand." Robin followed her

across the salon. "Just ask for me from the concierge. Madame Voisin. You know Madame Voisin?"

The girl did not reply. She was struggling with the lock.

"She'll send for me or take a message."

"*Oh Mon Dieu,*" the girl whimpered, turning to Robin with panic in her eyes. "The key won't turn."

"Let me try."

"Oh thank you."

Robin tried. To her surprise the key turned in the lock immediately and the door swung open.

"Thank God . . . oh thank God . . ." The girl rushed out into the corridor. She turned briefly. "*Merci, mademoiselle.* You saved my life."

"*Please* call me. At the pension."

"I will."

For a moment Irène paused and threw her arms around Robin. "Thank you," she whispered and Robin felt the soft warm masses of her hair against her cheek. Then she went tottering off in the high-heeled pumps, grabbing at her hair, which had fallen loose from its pins.

Robin watched her enter the glass elevator and vanish down the shaft, then, leaving the key hanging from the lock, walked across the hall to Suite 617.

She knocked on the door but Madame Gautier did not open it. She knocked again. Not a footfall could be heard from within.

"Madame Gautier . . ." she called and gave the door a good bang. Still, after the echoes died away, there was total silence.

Perhaps Madame Gautier had gone downstairs to eat some lunch. Or buy a bottle of Kaopectate.

Robin ran all the way down the red-carpeted staircase.

Madame Gautier was not in the lobby. Or in the shabby lounge or the seedy, odoriferous snack bar. Nor out on the rainy sidewalk. The desk clerk said he had not seen her since their arrival two hours ago.

"Well, if she comes in, will you tell her, please, that I'm upstairs in our suite. And by the way, she seems to have taken the key with her. Could I have another one, please?"

There wasn't another one hanging on the hook for Suite 617. The desk clerk said that the manager might have one, but he was out for lunch.

Robin had to wait until two-fifteen, when he returned smelling of wine and cheap perfume.

By then her anxiety about Madame Gautier had increased perceptibly.

"An extra key?" the manager asked, looking her over and sucking in his moustache. "Hm. I think we can probably dig one up somewhere . . ." Pulling a dirty cardboard box from under the reception desk, he pawed through it and at last dangled a large brass duplicate on his forefinger. "Voilà, mademoiselle. Would you like me to accompany you?"

"No thank you, monsieur."

Riding up in the elevator, she felt more and more uneasy. Why would Madame Gautier desert her post when she had instigated the entire expedition? The count's phone call and Irène's frantic reaction filled her mind with haunting conjectures, and the atmosphere of the hotel itself did nothing to reassure her.

The Hôtel de la Reine Matilde seemed more than merely sleazy and rundown. It seemed to emanate an aura of evil, as though it might be a headquarters for drugs. Caen was a port city, and port cities were often centers of crime. Perhaps it wasn't the hotel's low rates that had inspired Count d'Egremont to meet Quintana there; hadn't Guzman said Quintana was a drug dealer—one who would feel at home in such an environment?

The elevator groaned to a halt and she stepped out. The corridor was as poorly lit and silent as before. When she stuck the extra key into the lock, there seemed to be some obstacle interfering, and when she finally got the door open, she found that the obstacle was the original key. The door had been locked on the inside.

A chill like a cold finger traveled up her spine.

The salon was pitch dark. All the shades had been pulled down.

In mounting terror Robin stood on the threshold of the salon and called,

"Madame Gautier . . ."

No answer.

"Are you asleep, Madame Gautier? . . . Anything wrong?"

Asking these questions, she stayed rooted to the salon floor. With her heart pounding in her breast, she knew that she should bolt out of the suite into the corridor, run down the staircase, and summon the manager, but she didn't like him or trust him, and she had too much pride.

"Madame Gautier?"

She tiptoed into the bedroom.

It, too, was dark, but a neon sign in the parking lot next door kept going on and off, illumining it with bluish light every other second. In the eerie glow she saw Madame Gautier's dark-blue cape, her leather purse, and her plastic rain scarf laid neatly across the bed.

The bathroom door was slightly ajar and a sliver of light lay across the ragged carpet.

"Madame Gautier, are you in there?"

She heard the toilet running, and forced herself to push the door gently. It creaked and opened wider by itself in the slight draft flowing through the hall.

A single light bulb illumined the small room beyond and the bloody body of Madame Gautier. Sprawled on the floor with her head against the toilet bowl and her mournful eyes staring like two brown marbles, she lay slumped with her legs apart and her throat cut from ear to ear.

11

THE RAIN SPARKLED on the windowpanes of the Caen police station, giving a Christmasy atmosphere to the drab gray office, with its banks of files and fluorescent lights.

It was seven o'clock. Exhausted and fighting a throbbing headache, Robin sat in a chair opposite a somber young man in brown. His name was Inspector Jules Lefevre, and he was investigating the murder of Émilie Gautier at the Hôtel de la Reine Matilde sometime between the hours of twelve forty-five and two o'clock that afternoon.

A microphone lay between them. His voice was calm and impersonal. His gray eyes watched her from beneath their thick black lashes and from time to time he scribbled something on his pad. Behind him was a machine recording every word, and nearby, against the wall, sat a *gendarme* with arms folded.

"What was your relationship to the deceased?" Lefevre was asking.

"Good," she answered. "We were friends."

"How long had you known her?"

"About two days, monsieur."

"Two days?"

"*Oui.* I met her for the first time when I came to France

two days ago. Before that I had spoken to her a couple of times on the telephone."

"What was your purpose in coming to France?"

She told him, as she had already told him, about Madame Gautier's letter to her mother. And this led to the long, involved story of Marya's disappearance. It was a token of Inspector Lefevre's thoroughness that he asked the same questions twice, sometimes three times, as though he were trying to trick her into giving different answers.

"Why did you go with her to the Hôtel de la Reine Matilde?"

He had asked that too, but she replied dutifully that she had gone there in the hope of seeing Irène d'Egremont.

"And did you see her?"

"*Oui, monsieur.*"

"Before or after discovering the body?"

"Before, monsieur."

"Madame Gautier did not accompany you to the interview?"

"No, monsieur."

She had already told him that and given him the approximate times when she had last seen Madame Gautier at the door of their suite and when she had entered the suite with the key the manager had given her. He had also asked her if she had heard any strange noises from Suite 617, and she had told him she had heard not a sound at any time.

"At approximately what time did you return to Suite Six-seventeen from the d'Egremont suite?"

"I would say, monsieur, at approximately one-fifteen P.M."

"But you did not actually enter the suite until two-fifteen or two thirty?"

"Probably two twenty-five, monsieur. I had been looking for her in the lobby and elsewhere, and then obtaining an extra key to our room."

"Did you see anyone in the vicinity of Suite Six-seventeen?"

"No, monsieur. No one."

"When you were trying to get in the first time," he asked, "did you hear any unusual noises, like a scream or scuffling or faint cries from within?"

"No, monsieur. I heard nothing. Everything was quiet— as death," she replied.

"Have you any idea who killed her?" he asked. It was such an abrupt question and accompanied by such a sharp look from his keen eyes that she felt a twinge of panic. For, after all, presumably she had been the last person to see Madame Gautier alive and the first to find her dead.

"No, monsieur. I don't know why anyone would want to," she said. "As far as I know she seemed to have no enemies—although I know very little about her, except her name and address and the fact that she was a nurse."

"What was her address?"

She was sure he must know from the contents of Madame Gautier's purse or the hotel register, but she answered, "The Pension Bertrand, eighteen Rue de Grenoble in Rouen."

"Will you repeat that, please?"

Robin repeated it, he wrote it down, and then handed the slip of paper to the *gendarme*, who rose and left the office.

"What was the age of this woman—do you know?"

"No," said Robin. "But I would estimate that she was somewhere between fifty and sixty."

"Was she married?"

"I think that she was probably a widow or divorced. She mentioned a husband and her wedding, which had made her very nervous, but I never met her husband and she seemed to have lived alone at the pension for quite a long time. The concierge, Madame Voisin, said that she was her oldest customer, the one who had stayed there the longest."

"You say she was a nurse?"

"*Oui.*"

"At a hospital?"

"No. She had private patients. When I first arrived, she had just come from a case, and yesterday I heard that she had gone out on another."

"Did she discuss these cases with you?"

"No," Robin replied.

"Did she mention the names of any of her patients?"

"No. There was only one case she talked to me about," Robin said, "and it concerned my missing sister. She told me she had taken care of an old woman on her deathbed who confessed that she had stolen a child in a park by a lake in a foreign city. My sister, aged four, was kidnapped in Central Park near a pool in New York City, and Madame Gautier, who had read an article about my mother in *Elle* magazine, thought it was possible that the child stolen by the old woman was really her daughter."

"And *was* she?"

"I don't know. I've only met her twice but the resemblance is remarkable."

He fingered his black moustache.

The *gendarme* returned. He laid a slip of paper on the inspector's desk, and the inspector glanced at it, then looked quickly up at her. When their eyes met, he stared quickly down at the paper again, and for no reason she again felt panic.

But what did she have to fear? She was as much in the dark about the death of Madame Gautier as he was—and still shocked and revolted by the ghastly spectacle she had witnessed.

She would remember that bathroom and that body all her life.

But his eyes were upon her—sharp, impersonal. "Mademoiselle," he said, "are you sure that the Pension Bertrand in Rouen is the correct address of the deceased?"

"Oh yes," she said. "It's where I'm staying too."

"You are?"

"Absolutely, monsieur. We just came from there this morning. I ate breakfast there. I slept there last night. And so did she."

He shrugged.

"*C'est ça,*" he said, frowning at the slip of paper. "Perhaps it has some other name."

"No, that's the right one," she said. "It has the name *Bertrand* painted on the front. It's a queer little place hidden away in a sort of cul-de-sac. On the Rue de Grenoble, between two big empty warehouses. The street is so narrow most cars can't get through."

He listened impassively. Fingering his moustache, he laid the slip of paper aside.

Clearing his throat, he resumed his questions.

"When you left the deceased to visit Mademoiselle d'Egremont, did she seem upset in any way?" he asked.

"Not so much upset as very excited—in fact extraordinarily anxious that I should do well."

"Anxious—in what way?"

"Well, outside our door, just before I went across the hall, she begged me to be honest—*very* honest with myself. And then she kissed me, hard, on the mouth."

"Hm. Why do you think she did that?"

"I didn't know. It puzzled me. She had never really showed much affection for me before, and my first reaction was that—maybe—she was a lesbian."

"Do you think she was?" he asked.

Robin shook her head.

"No, monsieur. Not anymore. I mean I no longer think she was in love with me."

"Then what do you think the kiss might have meant?"

"I think," Robin said slowly, remembering the scene in the gloomy corridor, "that for some reason of her own, she was trying to warn me."

"Warn you—of what?"

"I'm not sure . . ." His gaze was so intent that she stared at her lap. "I don't know what she meant. The meaning was veiled . . . but maybe what she was saying was that . . . I shouldn't believe everything I was about to be told . . . or—something like that," she finished lamely.

"But did you believe everything you were told?" he asked very softly, with a certain edge to his tone.

And again sensing some deeper meaning in his words, she looked up and their eyes met and held for a couple of seconds. Then she said, "Yes—I did, inspector. I was thrilled by what Irène d'Egremont remembered of our past."

"*Eh bien. Vraiment.*" He sat back in his swivel chair, and for a moment his gray eyes narrowed.

Then, with a quick smile, he continued his questioning.

He asked her several more questions about her final encounter with Irène. Then he questioned her briefly about their two previous meetings—the scene at breakfast and the impromptu visit Robin had made to the fisherman's cottage.

He seemed very interested in the details of the phone call in the Caen hotel that had interrupted the magical moment when Irène had brightened so markedly at the mention of the names of the turtles, Benny and Sam.

"Did you overhear any of the conversation while she was talking over the phone to the person whose call interrupted your visit?"

"No, monsieur. She was in another room with the door closed," Robin replied.

"But she *said* later that it was her father calling?"

"Yes. And I think that it must have been, by her sudden change in manner. She was always very nervous when he was around."

"She didn't mention the fiancé they were supposed to meet at the train station? Whether he had arrived or anything of that sort?"

"No."

"Did she ever mention the fiancé to you during the course of your conversation?"

"No, monsieur. She only told me when I first came in that she was expecting a guest."

"Hm." He stroked his chin, which was lean and determined like the rest of his face. "In other words, your information about the fiancé came only from Madame Gautier."

"Not entirely. Some of it was supplied by Raoul Guzman," she said.

He frowned. "Who is Raoul Guzman? You haven't mentioned him before."

"A friend of Madame Gautier's," she said. "A quite unpleasant older man, a detective who has his own detective agency in Paris at the Avenue Molotoff. He took me to lunch yesterday and drove me in his car to Irène's cottage."

"*Un moment, mademoiselle.*" He held up his hand. "What's the name and address of this detective agency?"

"*L'Agence de Détective Privé de Guzman, Quatre Avenue Molotoff, Paris.*"

"*Merci.*"

He scribbled something on a slip of paper, which the *gendarme* picked up and marched off with immediately.

"Now please tell me more about this Guzman, mademoiselle," Lefevre said when the *gendarme* had left. "What does he look like?"

"He's stocky, middle-aged, gray-haired with a gray moustache, bold brown eyes, and rather coarse features."

"*Oui.*" He nodded. "What else?"

"His voice is loud and his expressions common. He talks like a hard-boiled American detective."

"Hm." He laughed dryly. "So—why did you go out with him?"

"Because I was looking for a detective to do some research."

"Why?"

"I wanted to find out some facts about Irène's background, and where she'd come from—whether she was really d'Egremont's natural daughter. I thought I was fortunate when Guzman showed up at the pension—"

"Fortunate?"

His voice was faintly mocking.

"Yes, monsieur. You see I know nobody in France. I was desperate for information. And when he offered to take me to Irène's cottage out in the country, I leaped at the chance. I didn't have a car. I know nothing about the roads. I have never been to Normandy."

"So he drove you to the cottage. Did he accompany you to the door of the hut and introduce you to the girl?"

She stared at him sadly. "No. He said he would wait for me in the woods while I went to see her. As I walked away I heard the sound of his car radio playing loudly. He had given me a police whistle to blow in case of trouble. But when Irène's father started yelling at me and trying to shoot me, and I blew the whistle, Guzman didn't come near me. And when I managed to reach the woods, he had driven away." She bowed her head and began to weep, not because of the memory, but from sheer exhaustion.

He sat watching her in silence.

With an effort she recovered herself and dabbed at her eyes. "I'm sorry, monsieur. It's been such a nightmare . . ."

"I would think so," he said softly. "But let's go back to Guzman for a moment. When he took you to lunch, where did you go?"

"To a very small café off the Place du Vieux-Marché," she answered. "It wasn't in the main tour area."

"Was anyone else there?"

She shook her head.

"Did anyone come in?" he asked.

"No one—except the waitress."

"And what did this Guzman eat?"

"Oh quite a lot. Quite heartily. Mussels. An onion tart. Plus half of mine. A lot of bread . . ." She could see Lefevre's eyes beginning to glitter. "And two apple pancakes . . ."

"Plenty of wine?"

"Quite a bit," she answered. "Two bottles . . . but monsieur—"

"And what kind of music did he play on his car radio?"

"Rock. At top volume."

"*Vraiment?*" His gray eyes were blazing. "I thought so."

"You *know* him?" she asked.

"*I* know him. But not as Raoul Guzman. Or any of the other names he has used in the past. Or even as the man you have just described to me. Except for the rock music. And the gargantuan appetite. Those are his trademarks, his unfailing give-aways . . ."

She rose to her feet. "I—I don't quite understand."

His expression darkened. As he opened his lips to speak, the *gendarme* entered and handed Lefevre a slip of paper. "*Merci,*" the inspector murmured, glancing down at it. He looked up at Robin and then handed her the paper. The letters danced before her eyes. They read "No Raoul Guzman or Agence de Détective Privé de Guzman at 4 Avenue Molotoff, Paris."

"Monsieur—" Her hand moved to her throat. The paper fluttered from her hand. Lefevre stood before her, fingering his moustache.

"Mademoiselle Chodoff, it's beginning to be obvious that none of the places or people you describe are real people with real addresses—but charlatans and imposters, including your murdered friend, the woman who called herself Madame Gautier."

"Madame Gautier? *Oh—non—non, monsieur!*"

"*Mais oui, mademoiselle.*" His tone was firm. "I'm finally beginning to realize that you've been victimized like many before you by a gang of swindlers, thieves, and murderers."

"*Murderers!*"

"*Oui, mademoiselle.* Murderers," he repeated harshly. "We call them in France the Terrible Kerenjis."

12

AS SHE SAT THERE staring at him, he explained that the Kerenjis were a small but deadly group of actors and con men led by a man named Guy Kerenji, whose real identity was unknown to the police since he was skilled at assuming many disguises.

"I suspect he may have played the part of Raoul Guzman," the inspector said, "since he is known for his big appetite and his fondness for rock music."

He told her that the Kerenjis specialized in swindling rich people who had lost a loved one they hoped might still be alive. "Missing wives or husbands are their favorite lures . . . or kidnapped children, like your sister," he said.

"They claim to have found the missing person," he went on, "and when the bereaved relative is on the hook, they produce a facsimile—for a huge sum of money."

"A facsimile?" breathed Robin, thinking of Irène's extraordinary resemblance to Marya. "But how can they?"

"By makeup, plastic surgery, and occasionally a real look-alike. In any case, unfortunately, they've been getting away with these deceptions for several years. The police all over Europe have been after them, of course, but they're sly and super-vigilant, and so far we haven't made a single arrest."

"And why is that, inspector?"

She felt as though all the breath had left her body.

She felt as though her sanity had deserted her.

"Why? Because we don't know what they look like—or who they are, actually, since they constantly change their appearances," he was saying. He sat down on top of his desk and reached for a pack of cigarettes. "So your clues, your experiences, your descriptions, will be valuable. And if you don't mind, I'd like to go over everything that has happened to you, from the day you first arrived in Rouen."

"But of course, monsieur . . ."

"The Pension Bertrand did not exist, of course."

"Did not *exist*?"

"No, mademoiselle," he said firmly, with a grimace. "It does not exist, and has never existed. There is no such boardinghouse as the Pension Bertrand on the Rue de Grenoble in the Rouen city directory. It's a fake address, a work of the imagination."

"But I lived there, inspector. I slept there. I ate there. It had a concierge, Madame Voisin, a cook, Madame Sophie, and a little boy, Jean-Pierre, who served breakfast, the son of the cook . . ."

He gazed at her sadly. "I'm sorry, mademoiselle. An abandoned factory exists at the address you gave me, but no pension. What you saw was an illusion . . . and undoubtedly the concierge, the cook, and the child were all actors, members of the Kerenji troupe, there to manipulate you, watch over you, and create a semblance of reality. But all were fake characters. None of them were real."

"Oh my God . . ."

She leaned back in the straight chair, closing her eyes.

She opened them again.

"You say that Madame Gautier was an actress?"

"*Oui.* Of course she was."

"But why would they murder her?"

He shrugged. "Perhaps because she rebelled at the system. She wasn't fulfilling her part of the bargain. Didn't you say she argued with Raoul Guzman?"

"Yes," said Robin. "Oh God—how horrible. You mean—he might have been afraid she was weakening?"

"*Peut-être.* Who knows the internecine workings of gangs . . . but perhaps she was beginning to feel pity for you."

"Oh . . ." Her gorge rose. She felt sick at the memory of Madame Gautier's kiss—and her gaping red throat. She put her hand to her breast. "How awful. Poor Émilie . . . but in killing her for her—her concern for me, then they had to put an end to their plot?"

The inspector nodded.

"I suppose so," he said.

"That explains the phone call and Irène's sudden departure?"

Again he nodded.

"So—Irène was a fake?"

"Of course," said the inspector.

"And her father, the count?"

"As phony as they come. He particularly sounds stagey, with that yelling and that violence. Stamping on your camera and swaggering about."

He stubbed out his cigarette and leaned forward, gazing at her pityingly.

"You see, mademoiselle, the scripts are all written in advance and Kerenji stages them. He's the writer, the producer, the director, and on rare occasions, the star, although I think in your case he might have played the part of Raoul Guzman simply to amuse himself. After all, he knew you were the daughter of a great actress and probably took a keen pleasure in deceiving you."

"How disgusting," Robin said. "But you don't know what he really looks like?"

"Mademoiselle, we don't know what *any* of them really look like. Some of the so-called women you saw might really have been men playing female roles. Madame Gautier might have been a man, although the autopsy will tell us, and maybe that concierge—what was her name?"

"Madame Voisin . . ."

"*Eh bien* . . . and that cook, Madame Sophie . . ."

"And the child?"

"Probably a midget."

"A *midget*? Oh no," Robin cried. "He was beautiful—and sweet . . . so pathetic and helpless . . ."

"*Peut-être* . . ." Lefevre shrugged. "But just remember that these people are artists, skilled performers, clever at makeup, impersonations, improvisations, all the arts of the stage. Your mother is a great actress and you've been around show business, so you know how a truly great actor can disguise himself so utterly that even his own wife might have difficulty recognizing him. Well—such is the caliber of the Terrible Kerenjis. When they're given a role, they change their appearance so completely that no one would know what they looked like to start with."

Robin sat motionless, her hands clasped on her lap.

It was all overwhelming and horribly frightening, and mingled with these shocking disclosures was the memory of the hideous corpse she had seen that very afternoon.

"So—now what will happen to us?" she asked at last. "My mother and me—who believed in all of it?"

"Nothing will happen—or *should* happen," he said, "now that you know about them and remain on your guard. But I warn you—" He slid off the desk and came toward her, his eyes somber. "I warn you, mademoiselle, that they don't give up easily. They may still try to reach you in some other way."

"And what would that be?"

He shrugged. "That would depend on Guy Kerenji's inventive powers. It would also depend on how great a fortune your mother possesses, and how desperately she wants to have your sister back."

"She *does* want her—desperately."

"Then you must convince her to restrain her feelings—or have every proposal made to her double-checked. Try to explain to her that she is in mortal danger if she even considers the possibility that your sister is alive and available for ransom." He took out another cigarette and tapped it on his palm. "I know this sounds harsh, but these people are ruthless. They prey on people's sufferings . . . on death and loss . . . and that's the cruelest kind."

"I agree," said Robin. "I'll do my best to convince her."

"Please do, mademoiselle." As she rose, he asked, "She has cancer, *n'est-ce pas?*"

"That's right, monsieur."

"May I ask you a personal question?"

"Of course, monsieur."

"When your mother dies, you will inherit her fortune?" Robin nodded.

He looked at her sharply. "It may then be," he said, "at that point that they will bring the greatest pressure."

"What do you mean, monsieur?"

"Irène, who looks so much like your sister, may come forward and claim half the money."

"Oh no. How could she?"

"She might," he said darkly. "It's been done in other cases. And if she does claim the inheritance and wins her lawsuit, I will have to tell you that it won't be long before you follow your mother to the grave."

"You mean—they'd kill me?"

"Of course. Without mercy."

Robin stood frozen. Suddenly she didn't want to budge, to leave his office for a moment. And where would she go? The pension was gone, and she had no clothes, no airline ticket back to New York—not even any money except for the pittance she had brought that morning to Caen. All her possessions had been left at the pension.

As though he had read her thoughts, the inspector said

he would arrange hotel accommodations for her in Caen until she was ready to return to the United States. And tomorrow he would see that she got back to the pension in the hope of retrieving any belongings that had been left.

"Oh thank you, monsieur. You've been extremely kind."

"I'm sorry this had to happen to you. But you've been very lucky," he said.

"I realize that. I was very stupid."

"Try to get a good night's sleep."

He walked her to the police-station exit and hailed a cab for her. He stood waving as she drove away, and she thanked God for Inspector Lefevre.

Morning dawned bright and fresh, and the inspector came for her and drove her to Rouen.

The breeze blew and the rain sparkled on the green fields and red poppies of rural Normandy. She talked to him about Jean-Pierre and wondered whether they would find him left behind at the pension.

"I *know* he wasn't any midget," she insisted. "He was beautiful, angelic, a most unusual little boy. And I can't believe he was the child of that boorish creature Sophie. I keep thinking he was probably some poor little waif they dragged in to give the place an extra dimension of reality."

"*Peut-être*," the inspector said. "But they'd still have to take him with them."

"Why?"

"He might talk, tell their secrets if they left him behind."

Robin sighed. "Then I'll never find him," she said, gazing sadly at the hedgerows.

"What would you do with him if you found him?"

"Adopt him," she replied.

"I see you love children," he said after a long pause. Then he told her he had two little sons of his own. One was four and one was two. "They miss their mother very badly." She had died, he said, in giving birth to the younger one, and the children were being cared for by his mother in Saint-Malo, Brittany.

"But it's not the same thing as a real family," he said.

All the bells of Rouen seemed to be ringing when they arrived. The Seine sparkled and the old peak-roofed houses and cathedral spires were bathed in golden light. Lefevre followed her directions and soon they were turning into the cobblestoned cul-de-sac. Ahead was the familiar squat shape of the Pension Bertrand, with the warehouses on either side and the wall looming behind it.

He had a gun in a holster strapped to his waist. He got out of the car first. Not a soul was in sight. A deep silence prevailed as he went into the tunnel entrance, then came out and beckoned to her to join him.

Still no one appeared.

The sign BERTRAND on the wall had been erased.

The gate opening onto the stone passageway that led to the lobby was locked. Above it, plastered on the wall, was a notice Robin had never seen.

CONDEMNED, it said in French. FORBIDDEN TO ENTER THESE PREMISES. TRESPASSERS WILL BE PROSECUTED TO THE FULL EXTENT OF THE LAW.

Lefevre stared at it without comment. "Do you happen to have a key?" he asked.

She still had the one Madame Voisin had given her. It fit the lock and the rusty gate creaked back. Beyond it, at the end of the stone passageway, she could see the glass door leading into the lobby. A huge piece of cardboard had been propped against it from the inside.

They pushed the glass door open. Lefevre kicked the cardboard aside.

The "lobby" had vanished.

It was nothing but a small whitewashed room. The furniture was gone and so was the wooden counter. In place of the winding staircase, a wooden ladder was propped against the wall.

"My God," she breathed. "They've gutted it."

"It looks like what it was—an old abandoned factory."

She kept gazing around at the bareness, the broom-swept cleanliness, the silence.

"But how could they work so fast?"

"They're stage people," he said. "Used to changing sets —moving scenery and props."

He walked out into the courtyard. It was nothing more than a strip of bare concrete, blazing in the sunlight. The pots of geraniums were gone and the dining room, with its café curtains, tables, and bentwood chairs, was merely a sort of open alcove off to one side.

"Is this where you first saw the girl and her father?" he asked as his shadow, long and lean, moved across the bare pavement.

"Yes," she said, remembering the thrill she had felt and the delirious hope. How they all must have watched her, and gloated over her reactions.

"And is this where Guzman appeared and asked you to lunch?"

"Yes, inspector. He was out here in the courtyard and Madame Voisin gave me his card."

"Of course he'd probably been there for a couple of hours. Lying in wait for you, so he could start his scene."

He kept looking around at the long, oblong hollow of cracked cement. "It was just like a theater," he said. "A little private theater. With entrances and exits onto the stage. This was one stage . . ." He gestured around the courtyard. "And the 'dining room' was another . . . and the 'lobby'—and your 'rooms.' All the actors probably lived here, hidden away perhaps in the basement, awaiting their cues, practicing their lines, rehearsing their gestures—all for your benefit, the scenes they would play for you. You were the audience, the sole *raison d'être* . . ."

"Disgusting," she said. "Oh, why didn't I suspect?"

"How could you, mademoiselle? You were isolated from the rest of the city. They fed you their dramas, inch by inch, and you had no one to tell you the facts weren't real. It was a closed world, a dream world, a perfect world of illusion and melodrama . . ."

Taking her arm, he led her indoors and over to the ladder leading to the upper story.

"Let's see if they've left your possessions intact."

The ladder was steep and long and very shaky. The rungs were wide apart. He told her to go first and he stayed close behind her, so close she could feel his curly hair against the back of her head and his warm, tobacco-scented breath on her neck.

"Just relax," he said softly. "Don't look down. Just look up and keep on climbing." He held her very gently but strongly, so she felt secure. She hadn't remembered that the winding staircase had been so high above the ground. But finally they reached a long, wide cement shelf extending across the whole upper half of the building. It was, it had to be, the "second floor" with its whitewashed walls and long row of rooms.

Not a sign of the wooden doors with their dangling brass keys was to be seen. Not a trace of the two rooms that she and Madame Gautier had occupied was visible—only crude, open, cavelike spaces hollowed out of the whitewashed cement with a few hingemarks showing here and there.

There were no windows, no partitions, no closets, no wooden floors.

The Kerenjis must have worked like a company of gnomes, toiling all day yesterday and on through the night.

Perhaps the moment it was decided to abandon the project and murder Madame Gautier for her softheartedness toward Robin and her possible defection, they had started dismantling the pension, their headquarters.

That was what the inspector thought had been the real motive behind the murder.

In any case, everything connected with Madame Gautier had disappeared.

Her pretty sleigh bed and oil paintings were gone. Even the outlines of dust that paintings leave on the wall had been smeared over with a whitewash brush and were already dry. Gone were the silk curtains she had always kept drawn, gone the damask chair, the rug, and the mahogany cupboard where she'd kept the wine bottle and the two wineglasses. Only a small heap of cigarette butts swept into a corner were left as evidence of the frizzy-haired, horse-faced woman who had been so superb an actress, with an all-too-human heart.

Robin's armoire, despite its colossal size, had somehow been spirited away.

Gone was her duffel bag, her silver comb and brush, her yellow skirt, underwear, linen blouse, and running clothes. And gone was the diamond-and-emerald bracelet engraved with the words LOVE ON YOUR 21ST BIRTHDAY, MUMSIE.

13

AFTER ANOTHER DAY spent in a flurry of activity, involving credit cards, bank accounts, and airline-ticket agents, Robin was finally able to reserve a seat on a slow, day-long flight from Paris to Nice, Madrid, and then New York. Only then did she face the hardest task of all—calling her mother and telling her the shocking news.

Four days had passed since that first happy call from Rouen after seeing Irène in the pension dining room. Her mother's state of mind must be at fever pitch—particularly since no calls could possibly get through to the pension.

Just before leaving for the airport, Robin phoned. From her Caen hotel room she heard the number ringing through. The voice that answered was Suzanne's, the Swiss nurse.

"Mademoiselle! Oh how wonderful to hear from you," said Suzanne in a guarded tone. And she said that Robin's mother had just dropped off to sleep.

"Oh good. Well, then, Suzanne, please don't wake her," Robin said. And glad to avoid the barrage of questions, tears, and hysteria she had expected to encounter, she blurted out her story to Suzanne's sensible ears. Suzanne was an intelligent person, a loyal, dedicated woman, who had been her mother's dresser and later her nurse since the onset of her illness. She promised to break the news as gently as she could. "But I feel she's already prepared," she said soothingly, "since we haven't heard from you since Friday."

Still, when Robin entered the penthouse after a long weary journey, she braced herself for an atmosphere of deep gloom and mourning.

She found all the lights on, music flooding the living room, and her mother up and dressed, having her face made up by Suzanne.

"*Hello*, darling." Smiling brilliantly, she turned from her dressing-room mirror. In the glare of its circle of light bulbs, her face resembled a painted mask.

"Hello, Mumsie." Robin kissed the top of her wig and hugged her. She could feel her mother's sharp shoulder blades beneath the thin silk blouse. "I'm *so* sorry . . ."

"Oh pooh. It's the name of the game, honey . . . the way the cookie crumbles."

Her nonchalance was belied by the smell of paint. As Robin passed the guest room, she saw freshly painted pink walls and rolls of new wallpaper. There were furniture cartons crowded into a corner. Obviously, after the Rouen phone call her mother had phoned a decorator and started preparing for Marya's home-coming.

"I thought we'd go to Leone's for dinner." Bewigged and bejeweled, her mother stuck her head in the doorway of Robin's room. "You remember Leone and his super-martinis." Robin remembered Leone well. He had been part of the glamour years of dazzling premieres and glittering first nights, when her mother, on the arm of some swain or other, had swept into his restaurant like a full-blown rose.

A stretch limousine arrived and they drove off in state.

Still her mother hadn't asked her a single question about France. On the way to the restaurant she was all gaiety and trendiness, discussing a new miniseries she had seen on television and a new way of eating called "grazing" she had read about. "I wonder if Leone's has caught up with grazing . . ."

When they arrived at the restaurant, her mother paused in the doorway to make a grand entrance, awaiting the stir of excitement that had always greeted her in the past.

There was none.

The restaurant had changed hands and Leone had retired to Florida, leaving only his name and none of his help.

They had to wait in line behind a horde of fashionably dressed young couples before a cool young maître d' deigned to lead them to a small table at the back.

"My, I wish I'd known," said Robin's mother haughtily. "It's become so déclassé. Just look at that chandelier. And this cheap tablecloth. And all these *drab* types. *Where* do they come from? Hoboken? Long Island City?"

"We don't have to stay," Robin said in a low voice. "Would you like to leave?"

"Oh no . . . we're settled now."

She ordered two double martinis—"one for me and one for my child" and a bottle of Dom Perignon, which she said she had no intention of drinking or "even taking home in a paper bag," but had ordered just to put that "twat" of a waiter in his place.

It was a sad indication of her mother's profound misery that she used coarse expressions, for she had always deplored the crude vernacular of the stage.

"So tell me everything about those assholes in France."

And:

"What kind of bullshits *are* these fucking Kerenjis?"

Her beautifully modulated voice, long accustomed to projecting dialogue to the farthest reaches of the second balcony, rose above the surrounding hubbub, and people at the next table stared.

"Let's talk about them later. Would you care for an appetizer, Mumsie?"

"No thanks. I loathe and *despise* appetizers. So *fattening!*" She tossed the huge menu aside and it fell, sprawled out on the floor. Robin picked it up. "I can't *believe* they're actors," her mother declaimed to the assembled multitude. "Actors are *decent*. They're basically *kind*." An eyelash fell off, and she waved it in the air. "These people have to be the shit of the profession. Otherwise the bastards would be working their asses off on some *legitimate* show instead of horsing around as *comic-strip characters*. All of them deserve to be hacked into little pieces and flushed down a Paris *pissoir*."

Out of the corner of her eye Robin could see a large woman at a nearby table leaning forward to her husband, and her equally large husband, with an irate glance over his shoulder, tossing down his napkin and pushing back his chair.

Their second round of martinis was brought much too quickly. "Let's enjoy these slowly." Robin smiled and toyed with her glass.

"Am I *embarrassing* you?"

In one gulp her mother drank hers down.

The waiter brought her a third. Robin waved him away. She asked the waiter to please bring their food as soon as possible.

Her mother told him to uncork the champagne before he left.

Her eyes had become glazed. She had developed a small tremor. She'd begun to slur her words. As the champagne cork popped, she leaned forward and said loudly, "You know, darling, I can't help thinking that she really *was* Marya."

"*What?*"

"That—Irène, you know. Who looked so much like me. You were *so* sure she was, that very first day."

She gulped her champagne thirstily.

"No—I wasn't—really."

"Oh you were—*so*! Don't kid me." Her mother's glassy eyes flashed. "You said she was my image . . . so—maybe what happened was—they *found* her somewhere—in a convent or someplace—and used her for their purposes."

"Oh—Mother . . . !"

"Why must you *argue* with me—incessantly?" Her voice rose in pitch and volume.

"Because," Robin said softly, "Inspector Lefevre said she was a fake."

"What dosh *he* know?"

"He's a policeman, an expert."

"But he doesn't know *her*. He's never *seen* my daughter. What ish he but some shitty-asshed French cop who's never been *anywhere* in hish entire life . . ."

"Mother . . . please . . ." Robin said, glancing at the large woman and her husband, who were still looking around in a state of outrage. "Let's go. OK?" She rose.

"But we haven't had our dinner." Her mother's head was wobbling. "I want your opinion firsht. Do *you* think she wash *Marya*?"

"I'll tell you in the apartment." Robin touched her mother's arm, but her mother struck the table with a small be-ringed fist.

"*Look*, baby," she shouted. "I thought about it all *day*, ever sinch Suzanne told me, and she's *got* to be Marya and nobody elsh. Because tell me. Jush *tell* me." She shook a finger at Robin, knocking over the champagne bottle, which began to spill its super-expensive contents all over the tablecloth and the floor. "Jush tell me how the *hell* they could reprodush *another* like me? I'm *unique*. I'm famoush." Again she struck the table-cloth. "I'm known throughout the world as *spesshial*. And they'd have to put back my ovaries and patch my womb together and get some *stud* to impregnate me before they got a DOUBLE!"

The maître d' was approaching, followed by the waiter and a man in a tuxedo. "We're going, we're going," Robin said. "I'm sorry. May I have the check, please?"

"We'll have to charge you for the dinners," the man in the tuxedo said. Robin nodded numbly and tried to raise her mother to her feet. By then her mother was a dead weight and her head with the bouffant wig all askew was down on the tablecloth, lying in the stream of champagne. "She's ill," Robin cried. "Will somebody please help us?" But not until she had paid the check and thrust an extra fifty dollars at the languid waiter did anyone come forward. Then, helped by the waiter and watched by an audience of unfriendly faces, she managed to get her mother out of her chair and half carried her, half dragged her out of Leone's and into the stretch limousine.

It took two or three days for her mother to recover. But she was so weak and depressed, she remained in bed with her face to the wall.

None of the medicines the doctor prescribed helped her spirits. She lost interest in food, books, crossword puzzles, even the music of her beloved Robert Schumann. When Robin turned on the Third Symphony, she asked her to turn it off. No longer did she lie on the terrace of a morning with her headset on, smiling at Arthur Rubinstein's version of the "Fantasiestücke."

"Just let me die," she told Suzanne and Robin in a plaintive whisper worthy of *Camille*. "There's no hope for me. I'm doomed. So let me die in peace."

The only subject that could bring any animation into her voice was her oft-repeated insistence that Irène was really Marya. She had a dozen theories—one being that the old woman in Central Park had sold her to the Kerenjis—or that the gang itself had kidnapped her and trained her for their purposes. She harped on these themes so incessantly that Robin phoned Inspector Lefevre, hoping to put an end to the arguments.

He seemed pleased to hear from her. "I was just about to call you," he said, "about your friend Madame Gautier. I've heard from the pathologist and she really was a woman."

"Good," said Robin, feeling relieved somehow.

"We've also traced her background. She was a minor character actress in her day, performing with a small theatrical company run by her husband. But her looks and atrocious temper were against her, and her husband left her for another woman. She was out of a job and penniless when Kerenji hired her."

"How sad," murmured Robin, seeing the long horselike face and small melancholy eyes and hearing the grainy voice berating Raoul Guzman on the phone. "I suppose she had no choice."

"She had plenty of choices, mademoiselle." His voice was suddenly harsh. "She was a criminal like all the rest." Then his tone softened. "Was there anything in particular you wished to ask me?"

"*Oui*, if you have a few moments to talk."

"My time is at your disposal, mademoiselle."

But when she told him her mother's theories about Irène, he showed no enthusiasm. "I'm afraid, mademoiselle, they're only wish fulfillment. In the first place," he continued, "it would seem a risk for the Kerenjis to use her. If she was your sister, she might remember you on encountering you and break loose from their control."

"But she was only four when she was kidnapped," Robin said. "She'd probably forgotten everything about us—and if she hadn't, couldn't they brainwash her?"

"It's possible—but not probable, mademoiselle."

"You realize," Robin said, "that these are not my arguments, but theories of my mother."

"I do, mademoiselle. But please assure her that in the years the Kerenjis have been operating, they have never used the *real* missing people as lures, only look-alikes. So it would be most unusual, against all their principles, for them to use your sister for the Rouen operation.

"As I told you," he went on, "they're experts at creating very lifelike facsimiles. They find somebody who resembles a photograph of the missing person and then send her off to be touched up in Romania or Switzerland by a plastic surgeon and a cosmetic specialist. The results are often remarkable, and have deceived several victims—so please tell her not to get her hopes up in that particular direction. What you saw in Irène d'Egremont, I'm quite sure, was manmade, not natural."

Robin drew in a deep breath. "Irène was also like my little sister in her mannerisms," she said. "It was one of the things about her that impressed me deeply—her shyness, her gentleness, the fact that she was easily led. How could they have known about those special characteristics?"

"By research," Lefevre replied. "When your sister disappeared, was there not a great deal of publicity in the press, on the radio and television, about the kind of child she was?"

"Yes, monsieur. A lot."

"Then—*bon*. You can be sure these people took it into consideration—and built the character of Irène accordingly." He cleared his throat. "And by the way, mademoiselle, I wonder if you'd be good enough to send me a report of that kidnapping. It might be of help in our investigations."

"I'll be glad to," Robin said. "I'll start getting it together. You've been so kind and helpful, inspector—and thank you for your patience. How are your little boys?"

"Just fine, *merci*. Enjoying their summer at Saint-Malo."

He was such a nice man, so decent and intelligent. But when she told her mother what he had said, her mother grimaced and said, "Dummy. What does *he* know?"

She turned her face again to the wall.

14

ANDY RETURNED from Hawaii and flew up from Washington the following day. They met for lunch outside a South Street seafood place. He looked handsomer than ever. His hair had grown longer and was bleached by the sun, and his face was deeply tanned.

"Robin, you look terrific." He took her in his arms right there on the sidewalk with the crowds and traffic going by. Seated above the sparkling waters of the harbor, she sat gazing at him, entranced by his tales of surfing on ten-foot waves, climbing extinct volcanoes, and sailing by moonlight in native canoes.

She felt young and beautiful and desirable again, part of the bustling city and the stylish young couples eating expensive lunches in fashionable restaurants. Later, in his hotel room, with the blinds down and the air-conditioner humming, they made love, and it was as wild and wonderful as it had been that rainy weekend.

If anything, he seemed more passionate, and, laughing, he said it was because he had forsworn many a bare-breasted Polynesian for her sake.

He was appalled when she told him of her experiences in France. "Good God, Robin, why did I have to be away when all this happened?" He asked her all sorts of questions about the pension and the plot that had been woven around "Irène" and her "tyrannical father." "Pretty corny and melodramatic," he commented; "but I suppose it was designed to make you feel sorry for her, so you'd pay some huge sum to the old man in return for her freedom—maybe buy him back his 'fiefdom.' " With a look of disgust he shook his blond head.

"I suppose so," said Robin. "But I believed every word of it." She sighed. "I was so dumb!"

"No you weren't. Just softhearted—as any normal person would be. And trusting." He frowned. "It's too bad I wasn't around. I'd have given them a run for their money. Though I can't understand why those French police haven't caught them by now. You'd think that after all this time they'd have figured out a way to bust their stupid racket."

"Maybe the Kerenjis are smarter than the police," she said. "And the police have worse criminals to worry about."

"Like who?" His blue eyes blazed. "Who could be more important to capture than those bastards?"

"I mean—all those terrorists," Robin said, "who've bombed department stores and shops in the Champs-Élysées."

"Yes . . . but the Kerenjis are also terrorists."

Robin sighed. She tilted her head back and let him play with her hair. He drew a long lock across her breast and kissed her nipples through its warmth. Her mind wasn't on the Kerenjis. All she wanted to do was drown in ecstasy again—in the languor of his hand stealing over her body and the moist urgency of his lips and tongue in the secret places of her being.

They lay spent and silent at last as the rush-hour traffic roared far below and the light slowly faded from the window blinds. Stroking her hair, which lay spread across his thighs, he asked quietly, "So what about us, Robin? What have you decided?"

She did not answer.

"Have you talked to your mother?"

"Not yet."

"Why not?"

"She—she's not in any state to be argued with, Andy." His hand moved away from her hair.

"She's very sick, much sicker, and depressed all the time."

"Because of me?"

"Oh no." She raised her head quickly. "Because of Marya."

"But is that fair?" he asked, still quietly. "Don't you count for anything? Your sister's dead, probably *long* dead by now—and you and I are very much alive."

"I know it, Andy, I know it," she moaned. "But my mother is my mother—and she's had a wretched time. Imagine—she still thinks that 'Irène' —that fake look-alike—was *really* my sister. She's obsessed with the idea, and does nothing but talk about it. So please understand—and let's just be patient. Can't we just go on seeing each other like this for a while longer?"

"I suppose so," he said, sitting up in bed with his arms wrapped around his knees. "But it makes me feel like some goddamn ghoul—sitting around and waiting for her to die."

"It's not like that. I don't think of it as that."

He turned to her. "Couldn't we just not tell her? She's too ill to even care. Couldn't we just drive down into the country tomorrow—to Jersey or Delaware—and stop off at a justice of the peace?"

"No, I couldn't, Andy . . . honestly."

"Oh for God's sake, why not?"

"It—it wouldn't really be fair. I've never deceived her in my life . . . and I'd feel too guilty. It's a matter of honor." She lifted her head and looked deeply into his eyes, "And I think it would get us off to a very bad start."

"Oh hell."

He forced a grin and shook his head, then got off the bed. "OK, darling. Discussion over. Sorry that I brought it up." He padded to a chair where he had left his clothes. He fumbled in his trouser pocket. "You see I brought you up this ring . . ." He came toward her with something gold and shiny, twinkling on his palm. "It's an old family ring . . . my mother's engagement ring, and I thought you might like to have it—as a marriage ring, in case we went tomorrow."

As he spoke, his fingers, coated with golden hair, curved and closed around the shining object. Then he turned and put it back into the trouser pocket.

"Oh Andy . . ."

He smiled at her over his shoulder. "Maybe later, OK?"

"Of course, OK," she said and held out her arms.

But he picked up his clothes and went into the bathroom. She heard the click of the latch. When he came out he was fully dressed in the blue blazer and gray slacks. "I'll wait for you in the lobby," he said. "I'm afraid we ought to have dinner pretty soon. I've got to be back in Washington by eleven."

He phoned her from Washington the following day, and that afternoon a beautiful bouquet arrived for her mother. With it was a card, "With best wishes and fond hopes for a speedy recovery. Andy."

Her mother frowned. "So you're still seeing him?" she asked.

"Yes."

"Well!" Her mother's voice hung in the silence. She studied the card again. "Very nice of him. Thank him for me." And she laid the card face down on the night table.

Robin took a step forward, her body quivering.

"Why don't you like him?" she asked in a constrained voice.

"I like him." Her mother turned her head away and plucked at a lace pillow. "I never said I didn't."

"What's wrong with him?"

"Nothing." Her mother shrugged her bony shoulders in the lace-and-satin nightgown. "I barely know him, so how could I form a judgment?" Her manner was airy. Delicately, she yawned, lay back, and closed her eyes.

Robin stalked from the room and went running through the blazing sunlight.

For an hour and a half she ran, creating imaginary confrontations and demolishing them. The fact remained that she did not really want to hear what her mother thought about him, or what arguments her mother might muster in defense of her own desire to keep Robin at her side, until at least the end of her life. Any confrontation would only lead to that, for she was sure her mother didn't have a thing against Andy, except that he resembled some old-time foreign move star.

Which was insane . . . ridiculous.

"And it's not as though I hadn't willingly sacrificed my whole life for her," Robin's lips moved, as she ran. "I love her. I've been happy to give up everything for her—and I pity her . . . but damn it—it's time the shoe was on the other foot."

The traffic rushed by and the river smelled dank.

"It's not Andy, of course . . . but only her own fear— of being left alone. And I suppose I could ask him to move in with us. But he'd hate it . . . every minute of it. And so would I. Our relationship would be ruined."

Andy called that night. Robin thanked him for his flowers, and her mother, hearing her talking, caroled from the bedroom, "Let me talk to him. Oh—helloo, Andy . . . what a sweet thing to do." But her voice had a false ring, and though he tried to be hearty and offhand, Robin could hear and feel his discomfort. After her mother got off the line they talked for another half hour, but it was mostly about how busy he had been writing a long report on his extensive Hawaiian tour.

There was no mention of his coming up or her coming down in the near future.

However, he continued to call every night, late in the evening, no doubt because he thought that by that time her mother would be asleep.

Robin lived for these conversations, the loving tone of his voice and the soft endearments he murmured. He told her of funny happenings in his office, and the problems he was having with his refrigerator and vacuum cleaner. He had a wonderful sense of humor, and even after she had hung up, she would lie in bed smiling at some of the imitations he had done of people he worked with—his boss and his prim old-maid secretary. But he never talked about a trip to New York until one night she blurted out, "So—when are you coming up, darling?"

For a second or two there was silence at the other end.

Then he cleared his throat and said from deep in his chest, "I was hoping you wouldn't ask, Robin. I'd love nothing better, believe me, but I've come to the conclusion we should give each other a little space for a while."

"Space? What do you mean?"

Her mind instantly leaped to another woman.

"I mean—let's be practical," he said gently. "It's not fair to *you*, darling, for me to be pressuring you all the time."

"But Andy—"

"And in a way," he went on, "it's not fair to me either. Because every time I see you, I feel frustrated as hell, and start to lose my temper."

"No you don't. You never have."

"But I might one of these days, and I know what it does to you—all that pressure and conflict. It's very selfish of me, and your mother needs you now, and I'm sure it's only a matter of weeks now—before—well, you know what I mean, darling . . . when—we'll be together for good."

"Oh—Andy . . ."

Her heart felt ready to burst.

"This is just a hiatus," he was saying. "Let's think of it as a hiatus . . . a period of assessment. And analyzing ourselves. OK, darling? Agreed? And I'll continue to call you . . . don't worry. We'll keep in touch."

"Then—you—you aren't coming up—at all?" Robin faltered, with tears starting in her eyes.

"Eventually . . . of course," he said in a cheerful tone.

"Although they're talking at the office about sending me to Montana."

"Montana . . . ?"

"It won't be right away, I'm sure," he answered soothingly. "So let's not worry about it. Any word about the Kerenjis and that French inspector overseas? Darling, *please* don't *cry*. It's the only sensible way to get through a hell of a situation."

The next morning more flowers came—an exquisite white basket filled with roses and delphiniums. But that afternoon he called and said his worst fears had been realized. They were sending him to Montana on an early-morning plane— to some remote ranger's station deep in the mountain wilderness. He'd be gone at least three weeks, but would try to keep in touch.

15

MEANWHILE, July had arrived. The hot weather began in earnest. She ran earlier and earlier in the day to escape the miasmic fumes of thousands of automobile exhausts, which turned the East River Drive into an inferno once the morning traffic began.

There were few joggers about, and the dry grass along the river was littered with trash and dog excrement. Oil stains and drifting garbage marred the opaque green surface of the river.

No matter how fresh she was when she started out, in less than ten minutes the sweat was pouring down her cheeks and neck from the green visor of her sun hat. Her black hair, tied back and twined into a long fat pigtail, flapped against her back like a wet club.

She ran without pleasure, ran only to keep her legs pumping, and her thoughts from her own misery, her disappointment and despair. For Andy did not call, and it was obvious that he was finished with her. Their brief romance had been ideal from her point of view, but obviously he was a man who wanted total possession of a woman—and could not bear even the slightest token of divided loyalty. . . .

Or else, somewhere in the course of his travels, he had

met another woman—someone more beautiful, more exciting than she—and was sending *her* flowers, calling *her* up.

For he did not phone her. He did not write—or send even a postcard. She tried to picture him in boots and khaki windbreaker, deep in a giant forest, or tramping up a mountain stream, or lost in a towering canyon, sleeping in a tent, and living out of cans . . . but nothing could mitigate her sense of utter desolation, her feeling that every joy she had ever found in her life, every golden apple dangled before her eyes, had been inevitably snatched away.

A week went by and then another. The days grew hotter. The heat rose, shimmering, from the scorching pavements, and sometimes on these masochistic mornings, mirages and illusions born of her loneliness and depression rose before her.

As she ran along the wide promenade above the river, she would think she saw one of the people from the pension approaching in the distance.

Fear had entered her world with the Terrible Kerenjis— and the inspector's prediction that they might contact her again. In the evenings she was gathering together the material on Marya's kidnapping to send to Lefevre, and as she read the old files, and went through the yellowed clippings, the horror of that Sunday overwhelmed her once again.

It had been so sinister a crime—with so few clues and such swiftness of execution. No reason for it had ever been found, no ransom note had ever been received. Nor had there been a single eyewitness, except for Robin herself, who could remember only that final glimpse of her sister slipping and sliding in her patent-leather pumps out of sight forever.

Lieutenant Feeney, since retired, had supplied her with a detailed report of the search that had followed. The park's larger lake, the Belvedere, had been dragged; so had the small duck pond lying below the path they had taken toward the zoo. Many park employees on duty that day had been questioned. A long array of sex offenders and child molesters had been rounded up. But the old woman, the soldier with one leg, the old men playing checkers, and the man with the poodle, as well as the two women who had stopped her mother and kept asking her questions, had never been found.

There had been no body . . . not a trace of Marya's clothing . . . ever discovered in the park or elsewhere.

Sitting in the heat and deep silence of the penthouse, she wondered once more what had really become of her.

Meanwhile, weird illusions and phantoms filled her solitary mornings. Walking along the wide sunny promenade past the silent apartment buildings, she would think she saw the figure of d'Egremont striding before her, outlined in light. Or, turning her head briefly, she would glimpse Raoul Guzman . . . and with heart knocking, force herself forward, till she was gasping in the heat.

Even as she raced wildly, fearful of stopping, and fearful of looking back, she realized it had to be a carry-over from the incredible reality of their performances in Rouen.

When Robin was a teenager of twelve or thirteen, her mother had starred in a mystery play that Robin adored, and night after night she had been permitted to watch it from backstage and see the actors come and go on their way to and from their dressing rooms.

They never spoke to her; they were too absorbed in concentrating on the parts they were about to play. As they passed her, she thought of them as ghosts who came to life only on the stage.

She came to think of them only in terms of the characters they played. And so it was with the people she had dealt with in Rouen.

Madame Gautier still seemed like a real person whose hoarse voice still rang in her ears. Full of vitality, she sat smoking on the edge of her sleigh bed or stood before a mirror, pulling rusty hairpins from her nurse's cap and tossing it aside.

The Pension Bertrand was still a real place, even though she had seen it stripped of all its furnishings. Madame Sophie still stood behind her square table in her butcher's apron, and Jean-Pierre, with his angelic smile, flitted about from table to table or cried out when his cruel "mother" boxed his ears. Irène d'Egremont was still real, no matter where she had really come from and how much plastic surgery had been done to her features. The sad expression in her beautiful brown eyes still haunted Robin—and the click of her high heels still lingered in Robin's ears.

These diabolical people had cast a spell over her that would not go away, in spite of all the inspector's revelations. They had been marvelous actors, trained impersonators and mimes who had played their roles so well that their "problems," their "relationships," however invented, would haunt her mind. Jean-Pierre, whoever he was, would make her yearn to rescue him, and Irène, no matter what her true background, would always be the shy, elusive, beautiful young woman doomed to marry the brutal drug dealer from Martinique.

In her loneliness, her melancholy, Robin knew that her mind was clouding. Strange illusions were entering it—but what was illusion, after all, and what was reality? In Rouen she had stepped into a kind of fairy-tale world, where all the values were black or white—and melodrama ran high, heroism and adventure were just around the corner. Perhaps only when all the Kerenjis were rounded up and the masks ripped off their commonplace faces, would she be free of their ghastly power.

On a hot steamy morning toward the end of July, as she ran down the steps leading to the Peter Pan statue, she saw "Irène."

She was sitting on a bench in the bright shimmering heat. Her brown-gold hair streamed around her shoulders and her delicate face gazed pensively at her lap. She wore a thin white cotton dress with puffed sleeves and a flounce around the skirt. It looked as though it had come from a thrift shop. At her feet was a shopping bag stuffed with clothes.

Robin stood midway down the flight of steps.

Irène looked up, and smiled timidly.

"*Bonjour,*" she said softly.

"*Bonjour.*" Robin descended the steps slowly. "What are you doing here?"

"Waiting to see you. Are you well, mademoiselle?" Her eyes were wide and full of fear.

"I mean what are you doing in America?"

"I came to see *you.*" She plucked at the white flounce.

"Where are the others?"

"*Pardon?* What others?"

"Your friends from Rouen. The count—and Raoul Guzman."

"Oh—I have no idea, mademoiselle. They don't know I'm here. I'm alone. I came alone." Her voice rose in volume toward an edge of hysteria. She was a superb actress.

"I'm sorry, I don't believe you." Robin turned her head and glanced quickly around at the surrounding shrubbery and then up over the facades of the neighboring apartment houses. Somewhere there had to be an observation post—with a telescopic lens, perhaps, even a tape recorder.

"But it's true, mademoiselle," the girl was saying in a tremulous voice. "I ran away. I was afraid of them, of what they did to that poor lady in the bathroom."

"I didn't like it much myself."

The girl rose from the bench. Clasping her hands in front of her, she said emotionally, "Besides, after our talk at the hotel that day I began to have these feelings."

"What feelings?"

Again Robin scanned the secluded park. She knew that it was a mistake to linger, much less talk to this girl, but at the same time she was curious.

"The—the feeling that I—I was part of your life," the girl faltered. "The feeling that I had known you—before."

"Nonsense."

"Please, mademoiselle. Hear me out. I—I have no proof, of course, except for the feelings you stirred up inside me . . .

when you spoke about the pony ride and the turtles and *Maman*'s dollhouse, where she changed around the dolls while we slept."

Robin listened, refusing to be moved.

It was Guy Kerenji's script and Irène was doing it well.

"It began to come to me," the tremulous voice continued. "I began remembering . . ."

She broke off and stared at Robin forlornly.

"What else?"

"It was like a—a *melting*—of my whole previous life."

"What else did you remember in this melting process?"

Irène gazed up at the morning sky. "I—I—" she faltered, then shrugged. "It's still not very clear. It's coming—slowly. After all, I was four years old when they stole me from you and *Maman* and I forgot a lot of things."

"Do you remember the kidnapping? The people who grabbed you?"

"*Non, chérie.* It's all a blank . . . a terrible shock. It was like a—a big wind swept me away and I was wrapped in a black cloak, and then I—was on a—a ship, I think, and someone else was taking care of me."

"Who was that someone?"

Irène shook her head. "I don't remember . . . and they say that I was sick for a very long time. With brain fever. I had brain fever, and it erased most of my memory. You've heard of brain fever?"

"Yes," said Robin. "They don't call it that anymore."

"Well, I had it. That's what happened to me, and all my past life became a blank," she said. "But when you talked to me that day in the hotel, it was like a—a *melting*." Smiling wistfully, she placed her hand on her heart. Her brown eyes were earnest. "So—I thought I would come to you. I had to see you again. And now that I'm here, I—I wonder if it's possible for me to see—*Maman*."

Robin stared at her stonily.

"May I?" the girl faltered.

"No. It isn't possible. Sorry," Robin said. Turning on

her heel, she strode to the steps. The girl gave a cry and followed. Robin turned her head. "And don't come back here anymore."

"Why can't I see her?"

Robin ran quickly to the top of the steps and hailed a taxi that was passing by. As she stepped into the cab, she glanced back and saw the girl standing where she had left her, with her hands clasped, looking up at her with an expression of anguish.

16

THAT AFTERNOON, while her mother slept, Robin put in a call to Inspector Lefevre in Caen.

He had just left for the day (it was seven-thirty in France) but could be reached, in case of an emergency, at his home in Saint-Malo. Robin said it *was* an emergency and gave the operator her phone number. In Caen the police operator said he would get in touch with him and ask him to call her back.

He called in an hour. In the background she could hear the chatter of little children. "What's wrong, mademoiselle?" he asked with concern. When she told him that Irène had come to the United States and lain in wait for her that morning, he muttered a French oath and then apologized for having used it. "I heard only yesterday that they'd escaped to Spain."

"Well, she's here, monsieur. And they've obviously been shadowing me. Otherwise they wouldn't have known about the spot she picked to wait for me. And now she's saying she's my sister, old memories have come back to her—and she's parted with the group and thrown herself upon my mercy."

"Oh *mon Dieu*, don't believe her . . . don't do anything she asks."

"Of course I won't, monsieur. But what shall I do about her?"

He was silent.

"Can I have her arrested, as an illegal alien?"

"I don't know, Robin," he said. (It was the first time he had called her that.) "I don't know the laws of your country, but if she got in with a legitimate passport, she's entitled to be there for a visit."

"She wants to meet my mother."

"Don't let her, whatever you do."

"She may try to see her in our house, when I'm not here."

"Then don't leave. Stay home, and warn the servants not to admit her."

"I'm also afraid she may try to phone my mother," Robin said. "And then I know my mother will want to see her—since she still believes that she's Marya . . ."

"Then make sure that someone else always answers the phone," he said. "Warn the servants. Can you do that?" he asked.

"Yes, Jules . . . but I know she isn't going to give up easily."

She heard something crash at the other end of the line, and a woman's voice. "I'm sorry to bother you, Jules," she said quickly, "but I'm desperate."

"It's all right," he answered. "*Alors*—why don't you perhaps talk this over with the New York police? Perhaps your friend Lieutenant Feeney," he suggested. "He might have some ideas . . ."

He sounded tired and distracted. A child was crying. Hastily she said, "Well, thank you, monsieur. I didn't mean to disturb you."

"My pleasure, mademoiselle. And good luck. *Prenez garde.*"

Lieutenant Feeney's home was not far from La Guardia Airport. It had evidently been built when the airport was a small one but now it lay in the path of a major runway, so at intervals the walls shook, and conversation was drowned out every time a jet landed or took off.

"People say I'm crazy to stay here," he shouted above the thunderous roar of a plane's arrival. "But I can't bring myself to sell it. It's my home. My kids were raised here and my wife and I had many happy years."

He was a handsome, florid man with a wonderful head of gray hair. He had put on weight since she'd seen him at the morgue with the drowned young girl, but he still looked fit. "Well, what's on your mind, Miss Chodoff?"

Robin noticed a large color photograph of her mother in nun's costume on top of the piano.

He glanced at it and smiled.

"Beautiful woman," he said. "How is she?"

"Dying," Robin said sadly. "But I want to make sure that it's in peace."

She told him the story of Irène's reappearance. She had told him about the Kerenjis when she'd asked him for data on the kidnapping.

"The inspector thinks you might know what to do about her."

"Let me think for a minute."

He lit a pipe and puffed on it as he sat in a big shabby armchair ornamented with crocheted doilies.

"My suggestion is to put a tail on her, and find out where she comes from, where she goes, and who she sees."

"Wouldn't the gang spot a tail?"

"Not if the job weren't done too obviously. If they're over here, she might lead us to them. And if they're not and she's operating on her own, as she says she is, then we could figure out some way to trap her and get her to squeal on them."

"We?" asked Robin.

"Of course." He grinned. "I'm going to be the tail. I'm getting bored with retirement."

For the next five days he followed Irène tirelessly, after locating her sitting near the statue of Peter Pan.

He wore various disguises—a blind man with white hair

and a beard, a drunk in longshoreman's costume, a fat woman with many skirts, and a subway guard in uniform. He kept his distance from her and mingled with the crowds, and he didn't think she spotted him. "She seems to walk around with her head in the clouds."

He couldn't get over Irène's resemblance to Robin's mother. "She looks like she stepped out of one of your mother's old movies," he said. "Those people in France have to be real artists."

He reported that Irène's mornings were spent wandering up and down the East River Drive or loitering near the statue, as though she were hoping that Robin would appear. In the afternoons she haunted the neighborhood around Sutton Place, the blocks adjacent to the penthouse, although as far as he could determine she never entered their building or spoke to the doorman on duty. Her nights were spent in the subways, rattling back and forth from dark to dawn on the Lexington Avenue line or the N train to and from Coney Island.

"Sometimes she sleeps on an empty seat, and sometimes she sits at the back of the car, depending on whether there's a cop on duty. She eats at juice bars or from street vendors. It's a terrible life. I don't know how she stands it."

"Does she meet anyone?" Robin asked.

"Not as far as I can see."

"How about in the ladies' rooms?"

"She doesn't stay there long, and I've watched from outside—you know their doors are kept open—but I've never seen anyone go in while she's in there."

Aboard the train, he said, there had been only one incident when she had been approached by anyone suspicious. He described them as a "couple of punks" who got on the train at Union Square and took seats on either side of her. Instantly she rose and moved to the rear of the car, whereupon the two youths followed, and standing in front of her, started pawing her breasts and her hair.

"She tried to escape, and I was just about to interfere, when a black man who'd been watching the whole thing got up from his seat and kicked one guy from the rear. When the other one turned around, he slugged him in the face with a very professional punch. Then they ganged up on him, but he was big and powerful—in fact he handled himself like an ex-pug . . . and it didn't take them long to back off. At the next station, they got out, and the black man disappeared into the next car."

"Did she thank him? Speak to him?"

Feeney shook his head. "No. Just sat there with this faraway look—like it wasn't really happening."

"Do you think she takes drugs?"

"I don't know. I doubt it. I've never noticed any of the symptoms."

"But the blank look . . . the apathy . . ."

"I think that probably comes from lack of sleep—or maybe worry," Lieutenant Feeney said, "that she's getting nowhere with you."

On the sixth day he reported that she had rented a room in a tenement on Tenth Avenue, inhabited mostly by drug addicts and prostitutes. He had also investigated her passport. It was bona fide, presumably. She had entered the country from Algeciras, Spain, on Iberian Airlines, and was listed as a citizen of France, born on July 15, 1965. Her name on the passport was Irène d'Egremont.

Marya had been born on August 2, 1965. Every year on that day, her mother had celebrated the occasion, and sick though she was this year, she rose that evening from her bed and donned a violet taffeta robe.

A cake had been ordered. Champagne was on ice. In the large gloomy dining room, seldom used anymore, plates and glasses had been set on the lace tablecloth and candles had been lit.

Robin and Suzanne took their places, while her mother proposed a toast. Gaunt and haggard in the flickering candlelight, she raised the exquisite Venetian flute. "To our darling Marya," she whispered hoarsely. "I remember when she was born, in New

York Hospital, that sultry night. Leo had a rehearsal and he couldn't be with me. I had just eaten my dinner, fried chicken, peas and carrots, scalloped potatoes, and chocolate cake."

She had been making this speech for the last eighteen years. Robin knew it by heart. "I wasn't expecting her that early, but I had barely reached the hospital, when—there she was. A beautiful fat baby with dark hair, lots of it, and never a cry—only a little soft *ech*. She was always so gentle, so little trouble, so—*good!*"

Her glass slipped from her fingers and she sank into her chair, giving way to sobs, as the candles burned, and Robin sat watching her, thinking of Irène in her furnished room just across the city. . . .

17

LATER THAT SAME NIGHT Suzanne knocked on Robin's door and said that her mother was having difficulty breathing. "I think we should get her to the hospital at once."

Pale and semiconscious, with an oxygen tube attached to her nose, her mother was taken in an ambulance to a West Side hospital where her doctor was waiting. After a brief examination she was placed in intensive care.

"It's her heart," said Dr. Cornstein, "a rather massive coronary. If she survives it, she'll have much less strength to keep on fighting the cancer. If she doesn't, then it might prove a blessing in disguise."

"You mean—?"

"Yes," he said, gravely. "It would spare her weeks of agony."

For the next four days Robin spent all her time at the hospital, waiting in a small, lamp-lit lounge for the brief visits she was permitted.

Her mother lay in a small room with glass walls, surrounded by machines. Her nose, her hand, and other parts of her body were attached by wires to various monitors that beeped and flashed. Her eyes never opened. Her breath came in shallow gasps. Occasionally a nurse with a syringe came and siphoned out the fluids that had collected in her lungs.

All Robin could do in the ten minutes allotted her was pat her mother's hand and whisper words of endearment.

During the nights, after her return to the penthouse, she spent the hours waiting for the phone to ring, or wrestling with the painful dilemma of Irène and her mother.

What was kindness, what was idiocy? All her life she had tried to make her mother happy. And the happiest thing in the world for her now would be to feast her dying eyes on the face of one she believed to be her daughter. But at what price? Happiness for the dying might bring death to the living.

Back at the penthouse, in her quiet bedroom above the glittering city, Robin paced the floor, wishing there were someone to make the decision for her.

Night after night she could visualize the scene in her mother's room at the hospital and imagine the radiance that would steal over her mother's face when she laid eyes on the girl who looked so much like herself and her long-missing daughter.

But then the words of Jules Lefevre would return to her: "These people are ruthless. They prey on death and loss. . . . And when your mother dies, Irène, who looks so much like your sister, may come forward and claim half the money. . . . And if she does claim the inheritance and wins her lawsuit, it won't be long before you follow your mother to the grave."

Sweat would break out on her forehead as she thought of Madame Gautier, lying with blood welling from her throat.

For a mere refraction of the rules, for questioning the authority of a Raoul Guzman, the Kerenjis had not hesitated to slash her neck in half.

And yet . . . in six days, according to Lieutenant Feeney, "Irène" had not contacted a single one of them.

Had she really broken away? Was she the innocent victim she said she was, or simply the tool of some scheming mastermind? It was so unfair. It was so very cruel . . . when her mother lay at the point of death and her peace of mind could be ensured in a few minutes.

Up and down the dark terrace Robin walked.

She gazed up at the stars and down at the rich dark-green shrubbery of midsummer, and prayed to her father for guidance in making this hardest decision of her life.

The days went by.

Her mother's condition remained the same.

And perhaps ultimately a decision would never have to be made. Her mother would die without regaining consciousness.

But her mother did not die.

One morning her eyes opened and she frowned with puzzlement. She tried to rise from her pillow and pull her tubes out. She spoke in clear tones.

"Where am I? What's this? Who are you? Where's Suzanne?"

By that evening she had been transferred to a private room and Suzanne was with her. Robin sat with them until eight o'clock, telling her mother all that had happened in the past ten days with no mention, of course, of Irène d'Egremont. Her mother was alert. Her keen mind had returned. She was very weak and tired quickly, but wide awake, almost her old demanding self, turning phrases and criticizing the hospital, even making jokes about her heart attack.

That night, while her mother slept, Robin and Suzanne walked down to the lamp-lit lounge.

Suzanne seemed dumbstruck by Robin's projected plan.

"Oh—Mademoiselle Chodoff!"

A thin sallow woman with gray hair worn in a crown of braids, she stared at Robin nervously through her glasses.

"You don't approve, Suzanne?"

"*Mais oui, mais oui* . . ." she answered hastily. "*C'est une idée merveilleuse*—but—theese girl, she is *not* your sister, no?"

"No. Definitely not," Robin said. "If I thought she was,

I'd have brought her home immediately, and told Mother about her long ago. And I'm only bringing her now because—I'm afraid my mother's condition is temporary. She may slip back into coma anytime, isn't that true?"

"Well . . . yes . . . it's—it's possible," Suzanne said sadly.

"It's inevitable," Robin said. "So—I'd like to make her happy before that—possibility occurs."

"But of course. Oh yes. You would make her divinely happy." Suzanne's eyes brightened for a moment. Then she sighed. "It would be a big risk to let those people even near you . . . but worth it, I suppose, at the end of her life."

"I agree. And I'm going through with it."

"So—when do you think?"

"We should do it soon. Maybe tomorrow."

"*Tomorrow?*" Suzanne gasped. Her sallow face grew paler. She touched Robin's arm lightly. "But may I make a suggestion, mademoiselle? If you do it, make this girl sign a paper, not to make any trouble for you."

"I was planning to."

"And—maybe hire a lawyer."

"Maybe," Robin said. "But I'd prefer to keep it private. Extremely private," Robin said. "The fewer people who know about it, the better. You understand . . ."

"*Mais oui.* And you can count on me, mademoiselle. I'll be quiet as a mouse. And I'll be there on duty tomorrow, of course . . . to keep the busybodies away."

Leaving the hospital, Robin took a cab down to Irène's dilapidated rooming house. But Irène wasn't there, so Robin scribbled a note and stuck it under the door of her walk-up room in a grimy hallway. She had scarcely returned to the penthouse when the phone rang.

"*Allo,*" said a soft voice. "Robin? This is Marya."

For a long moment Robin was tempted to hang up.

"*Allo . . . allo . . .* You still there, *chérie?*"

"*Oui,*" Robin replied grimly.

"How is *Maman* this evening?"

"Come on. Quit it," Robin burst out. There was silence at the other end.

Then a small voice said, "*Pardon.* I was just so 'appy to hear from you, *chérie.*"

"I'd like to talk to you, Irène. *Seriously.* In private. Can you come here tonight or tomorrow morning?"

"I can come *tout de suite.*"

"OK. You know the address, I'm sure. Take a cab and I'll pay for it. I'll meet you in the lobby."

After she hung up, she was again overcome by misgivings and a premonition of doom. But the wheels had been set in motion.

Irène paid for the cab herself and came into the lobby smiling. She wore the flimsy white dress with the flounce and the puffed sleeves, but even in this tacky getup, she caused a sensation among the help.

Victor the night doorman gawked and Gus the night security man looked as though he had seen a ghost. Neither man said a word but Robin knew what they were thinking—that some fantastic reincarnation of her youthful mother had just walked in the door.

She took Irène up in the private elevator and Irène acted very awed and overwhelmed. She was really a wonderful actress, performing just as she should—like a demure, naïve, simple teenager who had fled the gang and was overwhelmed by her first sight of the family mansion. "What a *beautiful* apartment." She batted her long lashes. "What exquisite furniture." The pointed eyebrows went up and down. "And you have a *terrace*! It's like a garden in Provence." It was nothing like a garden in Provence, but Robin kept silent. She led the way into the library, where only a few months ago her mother had upstaged Andy and ruined their romance.

"Would you care for a drink, Irène?"

"Oh no thank you. I don't drink," said Irène.

Sitting with ankles crossed and hands clasped on her lap, she listened intently to Robin's proposal.

"I would like this to be strictly a business arrangement," Robin said, trying to keep her voice from shaking. "I'm willing to pay you the sum of twenty-five thousand dollars in return for your services. All you have to do is act—for a few minutes—at my mother's bedside. I'll tell you what to say, how to act, and be there to help you. And if you do well, I promise to get you a screen test with a major motion-picture studio, because I think you're very gifted and could make a successful career in the movies or on TV."

Robin paused.

She could not tell what Irène was thinking.

"Agreed, mademoiselle?"

"*Pardon?*" She looked up blankly.

"Are these terms agreeable or do you have any objections?"

"*Mais non.* It's very generous . . . and I am flattered." She fluttered her eyelashes. "It just seems . . . a little cold between two sisters, *n'est-ce pas?*" In the silence she added tremulously, "As though I *needed* any compensation for being with *Maman.* That is why I came to America. It is what I'm living for."

Abruptly Robin rose.

"OK, Irène, then it's all off. Forget it." Feeling strangely relieved, she started out of the library.

Irène pattered after her. "But I *want* to see her— desperately, *chérie.* All right. I'll do anything. Just don't send me away."

Robin went back with her to the library, walked to the desk, and pulled out a sheet of paper on which she had typed an informal contract. In composing it, she had decided not to consult the family lawyer or even Lieutenant Feeney who had been calling every day to ask about her mother's health and what she planned to do about Irène. She was sure they would disapprove and try to talk her out of it.

"Here." She handed the paper to Irène. "Read this over, please, and sign your name right there."

"What is it?"

"Just a formal agreement with the same terms I've just described to you—the twenty-five-thousand-dollar compensation, the screen test, et cetera. It's for your protection when the job is done."

"I see."

Irène scanned the paper. She looked up, frowning. In a quavering tone she asked, "How is it for my protection, *chérie*, when it says I renounce any connection to the family?"

"Just what it says. You're to stop claiming that you're my sister."

"But I *am* your sister!" She jumped up. "Look at me. Can't you see that we're blood of one blood? I'm the image of *Maman*. I've seen all her old pictures and she looked just like me."

Robin picked up the contract.

"OK then, forget it."

"But how can I forget it, when it's all coming back? This city. I remember it. And you and me when we were children. I remember *Maman* and her dear face bending over me." Her voice rose hysterically. "Oh how can you do this to me, your own flesh and blood? What are you so frightened of, when I care for you so much?"

"Who wouldn't be frightened of you," Robin said, "when you're part of that gang?"

"But I've broken with them. I swear it. I ran away. They don't know where I am. And if they find me, they'll kill me— just for seeing you tonight."

Her voice, choked with emotion, rang through the room. Breaking off with a half-sob, she sank into a chair with her hands over her face. Robin could see her body shaking convulsively, yet still she remained unconvinced of the girl's protestations, her insistence that she was Marya, and totally divorced from the Kerenji gang.

Finally she said, "OK, Irène. You may be perfectly legitimate. But I still want an agreement that you renounce all claims."

"Oh—*claims*! Who cares about—*claims*!"

Her voice was weary. She rose and picked up the contract. "Very well, *chérie*, I will sign as you wish. May I have a pen?"

Robin handed her a pen.

Irène bent over the paper, then looked up. "How shall I sign it?" she asked. "With my real name or my false one?"

"The name on your passport."

"But that's false and you know it is. Irène d'Egremont! There aren't any d'Egremonts. And my name is not Irène." She turned back to the paper with a proud toss of her head. "I shall write the name our mother gave me—Marya Elizabeth Chodoff."

Elizabeth . . .

Robin had almost forgotten that Marya's middle name was Elizabeth.

But of course the Kerenji research people would have uncovered that too.

"I'm afraid Marya Elizabeth Chodoff won't do," she said. "Just sign it Irène d'Egremont or let's forget the entire deal."

Irène looked at her for a long moment. Then in silence she scrawled the name "Irène d'Egremont" at the bottom of the page.

"*Merci*," said Robin, and stuck the contract in the desk drawer. "Can you be here at five-thirty tomorrow afternoon?"

"*Oui*," she said dully, with her brown eyes gazing into space.

"What size dress do you wear?"

"Dress? Oh—size six."

"And shoes?"

"Five and a half—American style."

"Very good. They'll be here."

Robin walked her to the private elevator. When the car arrived, she stretched out her hand, but instead of taking it Irène tossed back her head, sweeping her long hair aside, so that Robin could see a small red birthmark behind her left ear. It was in the shape of a heart.

"*Au 'voir, ma soeur!*" She looked deep into Robin's eyes, and then whirled round into the elevator. Robin's heart was pounding by that time, but then she remembered that plastic surgery could accomplish wonders. The Kerenjis had thought of everything. . . .

18

AT SEVEN-THIRTY the following evening they set off for the hospital.

It was a ride that would take approximately half an hour at that time of night by the route Robin invariably asked all cab drivers to follow—one that avoided having to cross Central Park, a place for which she still felt the keenest aversion and had not entered for eighteen years.

Irène looked exquisite in the soft blue dress Robin had bought her in a Madison Avenue boutique that morning. It was fashionable yet simple, with long sleeves and a high neck, a flowing dress reminiscent of an angel's robe.

With her long wavy hair parted in the middle and her delicate coloring, she resembled a Christmas-tree angel.

She sat back against the leather seat of the cab, with her feet, in high-heeled blue linen pumps, tucked under the folds of her long sweeping skirt, as they drove west up Fifty-seventh Street, turned right into Columbus Circle, and then started uptown along Central Park West. From time to time she closed her eyes as though she were saying a prayer.

Visiting hours, which ended at eight, were over by the time they reached the hospital. The corridors were deserted and a general hush prevailed. However, due to her mother's celebrity, the hospital staff was inclined to be lenient about rules and regulations. As they crossed the marble lobby, the receptionist greeted them pleasantly and waved them toward the elevator. On her mother's floor the nurse's station was deserted, probably because most of the nurses were busy putting their patients to bed.

Above all things Robin wanted to avoid encountering anyone from TV or the newspapers. Ever since word had gotten around that her mother was a patient at the hospital, members of the media had been haunting the halls and asking questions of the staff.

But at this hour they met no one.

She took Irène's arm as they came toward her mother's door at the end of the long corridor. Irène was trembling. She kept wobbling along in her tight new pumps and her high heels clicked on the shiny waxed linoleum.

Her mother's door was closed.

Posted on it was a sign, OXYGEN IN USE. NO VISITORS. Robin knocked on the door, expecting to see Suzanne, and when no one appeared, turned the knob, prepared to walk in.

The door was locked.

She knocked again. The door was opened by a hard-faced nurse with bleached-blond hair and horn-rimmed spectacles.

"Sorry, miss. Visiting hours are over," she said.

"But I'm her daughter," Robin said. "Where's Suzanne, her regular nurse?"

"She doesn't have the proper credentials. The doctor said he wanted a *registered* nurse."

"That's odd. He didn't mention it to me. And she's been taking care of my mother since she entered the hospital. The doctor should have called me."

"That's not my business," the woman replied, and she started to close the door.

"Now, just a minute," Robin said, sticking her foot in the door before it closed. "I'm her daughter and this young lady has come a long way to see her. So let us in right now, please

—or I'll have to report you to the head nurse for unprofessional behavior."

"I'll speak to her myself," said the woman tossing her head. "And see if *she* approves of breaking the rules."

"Do that," said Robin. "And send her in to me, please. And don't come back yourself until I've talked to her."

The woman glared at her through her owlish spectacles, then, shrugging her shoulders huffily, stalked away down the corridor.

As Robin stared after her furiously, Irène touched her sleeve.

"Come, *chérie*. Let's not waste time. Let's go in while we have the chance."

She pushed the heavy door open and slipped inside the lamp-lit room, and Robin followed. The odor of flowers was like that at a funeral parlor. In the center of the room was a hospital bed on which lay a small childlike figure.

A floor lamp draped with a towel cast subdued light on the bare white walls and turned to silver the sparse aureole of hair resting on the pillow. Her mother lay sleeping on her side with her knees drawn up in a fetal position. A green oxygen tube trailed from her nose to the wall and other tubes hung from bags of glistening solution.

Her breathing was light and shallow. The bones of her cheeks and her small upturned nose seemed carved out of ivory. As Robin approached the bed, and Irène hung back, not far from the door, her mother's face appeared to be the face of a corpse, someone beyond all caring, someone no human emotion would ever stir.

But she was still alive.

The two women stood quietly and waited.

For several moments there were only the sounds of her mother's faint breathing, the hiss of oxygen, the click of machines, and the subdued tread of rubber-soled feet passing in the corridor.

Her mother stirred.

She turned over on her back with difficulty, opened her dazed eyes, stared emptily at the ceiling, then closed them again.

"Mother darling . . ."

Robin touched the clammy cheek.

Her mother sighed. As though trying to drag herself back from some far country, she moved her head to and fro on the pillow. Her eyelids fluttered. Then her hand emerged with the wrist encumbered by bandages and tubes and began twitching along the hem of the white sheet in an ominous fashion. Robin's heart sank. Since childhood, "plucking at the sheets" had been a phrase associated in her mind with approaching death.

"Mother . . ." She bent over the unconscious form.

Her mother heard. She opened her eyes wide and gazed around, startled.

Her eyes looked enormous. They hung in her face like wilting lavender pansies. Still surrounded by a dark fringe of thick lashes, they were clouded with drugged sleep, but gradually their expression cleared, and they focused and brightened.

"*Robin . . .!*" she whispered, and her voice was like the rustle of tissue paper.

"Oh Mother . . . oh dearest Mother . . ." Robin enfolded the slight body in her arms. "How are you? Feeling better?"

Her mother smiled faintly, and in the smile was all the weariness and despair of her long, painful ordeal. Robin glanced back at Irène, who was standing silent and motionless in the shadows at the back of the room beyond the circle of lamplight.

"Mother," she said. "I've brought someone with me."

"Who?"

"Someone I'm sure you'll be very glad to see."

"Who?"

Robin nodded to Irène. Silently the girl came forward to the foot of the bed in her blue dress, with her cloud of brown hair shining around her shoulders.

"Here she is," Robin said softly, finding it difficult to speak for the lump in her throat. "Recognize her?"

Her mother raised her head slightly. She stared across the white expanse of sheet at the angelic figure standing at the foot of the bed, and for a moment, judging by her look of disbelief and confusion, her clouded mind must have leaped to the conclusion that she had died and this was a vision come to lead her to heaven.

"*Maman*," whispered Irène.

The vague eyes focused and widened and blinked.

"Crank me up!" she gasped, as she struggled to rise from her tangle of tubes. As Robin hastened to the side of the bed and pressed the electric button, she could see her mother's expression change from bewilderment to awe, and then her lips began to quiver and tears filled her eyes.

"Oh my God . . . my God," she breathed, still staring at the beautiful young figure standing at the foot of the bed. "Oh dear God . . . oh no . . . it can't be . . ." Her voice broke, and she began to weep with wrenching, convulsive sobs. Then, half dragging herself upright, she tried to extend her skeletal arms in the hospital gown.

"You remember me, *Maman?*" Irène moved to her quickly and took her gently in her arms. "It's Marya."

"Oh dear God . . ."

Clinging to Irène and trembling on the half-raised bed, the dying woman could utter only broken cries and wracking sobs.

"Do you remember me, *Maman?*"

"Oh—oh yes . . . dear God . . . oh yes."

"I'm Marya, *Maman* . . . come back to you from France." Irène sat on the bed beside her and stroked the wisps of sparse gray hair. "I've searched all over to find you, *Maman* . . . and I've missed you so." Her voice caught and she bowed her head.

"And I've missed you too, my darling." It was pitiful to hear the plaintive voice, as weak and vulnerable as a little child's, and yet so painful to know that the joy and love from which it sprang were all based on a lie.

"But—but how did you escape them? Those wicked people?"

"It doesn't matter . . . I found you, and I'm here." Irène said in her heavily accented English. "And we're never going to be parted again—*ever . . .* !"

"Oh no . . . oh dear God. Oh—you're still so beautiful." The mother reached up and stroked Irène's hair. "Just as you were when you were a baby. You haven't changed . . . No . . . not a bit . . . Just as sweet and lovely—and gentle—as ever."

"*Merci, chère Maman.*"

Irène drew her close and kissed her. And she was playing it beautifully, Robin thought. Like the real pro she was, able to improvise a scene once she knew what was wanted and end up almost believing that she *was* the person whose part she was playing.

Her mother had been an actress like that. In fact, her ambition in her palmy days might have been to play just such an emotionally charged situation. She would have done it to the hilt, and for a moment, looking at the two faces side by side on the pillow, Robin had the strange illusion that Irène *was* her mother as a young woman, the mother she remembered walking beside her in Central Park that morning, and then sobbing on the pavement as though her heart would break.

But now her mother was dying, and nothing had *really* come full circle. Suddenly Robin felt sick with disgust at the cheatery she had engineered and she longed for someone to enter the room and put a stop to it.

Instead, with Irène's hand held tightly in her own, her mother was looking more and more ecstatic. Her eyes had brightened. A flush had come into her wasted cheeks. In the glow of the lamplight it was even as though some echo of her old beauty had returned to her face and once-melodious voice.

"Oh my darling," she was saying, "is there anything in the past we had together you remember . . . any little thing . . . ?"

"*Mais oui,*" Irène's soft voice was answering—and its

lilt bore an eerie resemblance to the older woman's. "But of course . . ."

The mother smiled. "What do you remember about us?"

"Oh many things . . . small things . . ."

"Like what, dearest?"

"Oh . . . my . . . my dollhouse . . . and the dolls you used to change around when we were sleeping."

As though asking for help, for Robin to come to the rescue, her eyes met Robin's across the long narrow bed.

"Oh yes." Her mother's laugh sounded joyously. And when had been the last time she had heard her mother laugh like that? "I'd forgotten that," she said. "And what else, my love?"

She placed Irène's hand on her bony white arm and began to stroke it. Her huge eyes were bright with a translucent serenity.

"Oh . . . let me think." Color flooded Irène's face. "I —remember," she began to stammer as Marya had stammered whenever a direct question was put to her by a stranger. "I—I —remember our t-turtles . . . the—t-turtles . . . B-Benny . . ."

"You *do*?" interrupted the mother wildly. "Oh yes . . . the tuttles. I'd completely forgotten them."

"One was g-green and p-purple . . ." Irène slid her hand away and turned to Robin with a vague bemused expression. For an instant it was as though she were looking past them both, past the room and the entrapment of their silent watchful faces. "B-but B-Benny d-died . . . 'and—um—um—D-Daddy b-bought me Zumgolly . . ."

She burst into tears.

With her hands over her face, she sat rocking back and forth on the hospital bed.

Robin stood pale and aghast, watching Irène's tears dripping through her fingers, glistening in the lamplight.

Where had the Kerenjis found out about Zumgolly?

No mention of the name had been made in the briefing or in anything she had told Irène. It was an obscure, crazy name

Marya herself had thought up—long ago, in fact, so obscure that Robin had long since forgotten it—till it leaped from Irène's lips, bringing with it poignant memories of the toy closet, the scruffy brown monkey, and her sister sitting on the floor of the nursery, squealing "Chee—chee—chee . . . " naughty Zumgolly—chee."

Was Irène her sister? Or had some researcher found the name in some old fan magazine?

Her heart seemed to stop beating, as she stood swaying in the shadows, and then footsteps thundered outside in the hall, and a troop of people burst through the open door.

"Hi. We're from *Night Beat*." They wore T-shirts and jeans, trendy hairstyles and beards. She had never seen them before, in the halls or otherwise. Bearing cameras and trailing wires, they commandeered the sickroom, rushing up to the head of the bed and forming a wall around her recumbent mother and the figure of Irène seated beside her.

"Hello! We just heard some great news," someone said, as Robin rushed forward and tried to push them aside. "You've found your missing daughter, right?"

"No. Get out of here!" Robin could scarcely speak. "It's none of your business . . ." Rage choked her voice.

She flailed her arms at them, but nobody budged.

"Do something!"

She turned. The blond nurse had entered, buxom and owlish. "Get these people out of here. Who let them in?"

"They're the press, honey," the woman answered, in her sneering husky voice. "Reception gave them permission."

"Well tell reception to drop dead."

But it did no good. They had formed a tight phalanx around her mother's bed. They were pointing their microphones and bringing their cameras closer.

"Lights!" someone yelled. And blinding floodlights filled the sickroom.

"Stop it. Leave her alone!" Robin shouted, but the blond nurse grabbed her and tried to shove her into the corridor.

"How dare you. She's my mother." Robin kicked her in

the shin. And for a moment she was tempted to tell the truth, scream it to them all. If she didn't, then tonight, by midnight at the latest, the news of Irène's reappearance would be on every network in the country. . . . Irène officially would become Marya Chodoff, without any further proof. Her heart sank and her stomach churned as she heard her poor mother's faint voice from the head of the bed.

"Oh yes," her mother was saying, "she's my dear dear little daughter come back to me at last. And tonight I feel I'm the luckiest woman in the world." Her voice faltered and trailed away. Then, as the cameras clicked and the lights grew hotter and hotter, the tremulous voice resumed at a slightly stronger volume. "You see—for eighteen years I prayed to God to bring her back to me. And now, I'm going to pray to Him to let me live a little while longer . . ."

Tears blinded Robin's eyes, and she knew that no matter what the real truth was, she could never destroy that beautiful illusion. This was the supreme moment of her mother's life, and she, Robin, had brought it about, and now, for as long as her mother lived, she must go along with the illusion, keep silent, and endure whatever falsehoods might be ballyhooed in the press.

Only with the death of her mother would she be able to make sure who Irène really was—and what her motives were, and whether the Kerenjis were still controlling her.

As Robin stood there at the back of the room, listening to the mawkish questions the interviewers were asking and the timid answers Irène was faltering out, she noticed a blond bearded youth in a gray running suit who was watching her from the doorway. Leaning on one elbow, he caught her eye and grinned and the grin seemed familiar—and strangely sinister. "You the older one, right?"

She did not answer.

"Like to make a statement for our midnight edition?" He took a step closer. A finger jabbed her in the ribs.

"No." She glared at him. "Get lost."

"Whatsa matter? Jealous?"

As he grabbed her arm, she jerked loose and spat at him. His pale blue eyes popped angrily, and then with a plummeting heart, she realized where she'd seen him last. Standing behind a white tablecloth in a butcher's apron and pink hair curlers, pouring coffee at the Pension Bertrand.

With a scream she dodged away from his tall wiry body. The blond nurse stood, arms akimbo, in her path. But elbowing her way out into the corridor, she raced down the length of slippery floor, knowing she had no choice, no hope except to run, run like the wind.

19

FLEEING ALONG the waxed gray linoleum and racing, two steps at a time, down four flights of service stairs, she reached the lobby and pushed the door open. Fortunately it had not yet been locked.

A cab was waiting in front of the main entrance under the porte cochere.

At the wheel was a kindly-looking old fellow with a red face and a circlet of white hair. He wore a brown sweater.

Robin hurled herself in and slammed the door. She locked both doors.

"Fifty-seventh Street and Sutton Place, please," she gasped, breathing hard. "And I hate to rush you, but I'm in a terrific hurry."

"Sure, lady. OK to go through the park?"

"Oh no . . . no, please. Straight down Central Park West to Columbus Circle, if you don't mind. Then east on Fifty-seventh Street."

"OK, but the park's quicker . . . if speed is what you're after."

"It's not that important," she said. "I'm just not crazy about the park. All those dark roads."

"I know what you mean, lady," he laughed wheezily.

They started off. A sticky breeze blew in. The night was hot and humid, and as they passed the Museum of Natural History she saw a flicker of lightning.

At Seventy-second Street they stopped for a traffic light. To their left was an entrance into the park, and as soon as the light changed, the cab shot into it.

"Just a minute, driver . . ."

She rapped on the glass partition. "Not this way, please," she called. "I want to go by way of Columbus Circle . . . and East Fifty-seventh."

He did not seem to have heard. He kept driving deeper into the park, down a dark winding road lined with stone walls and spanned with stone bridges.

"Stop. Please. *Stop!*"

Leaning forward, she could see small piglike eyes in the rearview mirror. His cheeks were pudgy and very red. It was the face of Madame Voisin.

In that instant the cab spun around in a sharp U-turn and he sped back toward the West Side again. But before he reached Central Park West, he turned right, crashing into a small lane ending in thick underbrush. The cab jolted to a halt.

Immediately she unlocked the door, but he was already out of the driver's seat and coming toward her. His tufts of white hair loomed up on her left, and he was smiling at her, with a long thin knife in his hand.

"Oh my God, my God . . ." She dived for the door on the other side, but it was locked and he had already opened the one on her left. There was no time to escape, no time to do anything but face him and try to fend him off, and she tried to think of weapons—the atomizer in her purse? A nail file? But neither of these would prove very effective. And then she thought of her high-heeled shoes, and she slipped the right one off and reached down for it.

As he squeezed his big bulk into the back of the cab, she pretended to cower, and drew back her arm. With all the force she could summon, she thrust the steel tip of the pump as close to his right eye as she could. It missed, but the blow was enough to make him grunt, slap his hand to his cheek, and stagger back from the open door. In a flash she was out of the cab on the other side and stumbling through underbrush. He grabbed at her skirt but she darted off, kicking off the other shoe as she ran.

Blindly, with every ounce of adrenaline pumping strength into her body, she ran as though the hounds of hell were after her, into the park she had feared for so long.

She struck out across what appeared to be a dark rolling meadow dotted with trees and boulders. Her eyes searched the darkness for a police car or a patrolman.

Ahead, looming against the black clouds of the gathering storm, was a misty wall of lights that must be Fifth Avenue. And behind her, looking equally remote, were the floodlit towers of Central Park West.

The lightning flashed. In its fitful glare the terrain around her was filled with eerie shadows. Glancing back, she saw him coming at her from behind a bush. One hand was rubbing his face and the other was brandishing the knife.

She started running toward the dim lights of Fifth Avenue, wondering why the park was so empty of people.

Where were the police? The lovers? The muggers she always read about in the newspapers?

"Oh God . . . please make somebody be here."

She dared not cry out or yell for help for fear that "Voisin" would find her in the dark.

But at least she had one advantage over him. He was fat and middle-aged and asthmatic, while she was young and a seasoned runner.

Even as she was flattering herself on her own athletic prowess, a pair of headlights blazed out of the darkness. The cab was following her across the meadow.

"Help! *Help!*"

Heading for the nearest boulder, she darted behind it and crouched low. On the lights came, flooding the terrain with fierce white light. She heard him stopping and getting out—and fled the boulder for open ground. Where could she go? Where could she possibly hide? All she could do was try to find steeper ground with a sharp enough incline that the cab couldn't negotiate— nor could he too easily.

In the next lightning flash she spied a rocky hill perhaps a hundred feet ahead, with a grove of trees topping its summit. Gathering her strength, she raced for it, and reaching it, scrambled upward on her hands and knees. The meadow grass turned to earth and pebbles. Sharp-pointed stones tore at her feet. Her panty hose were already torn and she felt as though she were walking on knives. But the headlights had stopped coming. They were dim blurs in the darkness. Blessedly she reached the grove of trees and, sobbing with relief, threw her arms around the nearest tree trunk.

Never in all her years of running had she driven herself so hard.

She longed to rest. It was impossible to rest. For she knew that the gang would not give up easily. Soon Voisin—and no doubt Sophie—would be upon her like a pair of wolves. Limping through the trees, she jogged on desperately.

A lake stretched below, glimmering with a lurid sheen in the intermittent lightning. She glimpsed moored rowboats and a bridge spanning misty water. Beyond the rowboats and the bridge was a large building and a parking lot.

Beyond the bridge she thought she could see the rotating green-and-red lights of a patrol car.

She raced downhill toward the lake.

Dry leaves rustled under her and pebbly shale slid from her feet. The lake looked large and strangely unreal, a horror-story tarn, rimmed with mist and surrounded by trees. The bridge that spanned it was equally haunting, a strangely wrought old iron bridge of another era with a flooring of wooden planks.

As she stepped out on it, she heard weird laughter.

Halfway across she stopped dead still.

For the laughter had sounded again, high-pitched and unearthly. Perhaps it was a bird calling from its cage in the zoo. Then she saw a light floating slowly toward her from the moored rowboats, a glowing orange light like a Japanese lantern. Bobbing across the still lake, with its orange reflection mirrored in the water, a tiny barge with a lantern at its prow moved toward the bridge.

On it was set a child's small white coffin lined with satin and containing the body of a small child. As the craft came closer, Robin saw that the figure was a perfect reproduction of Marya as she had looked at the age of four. She was dressed as she had been dressed on the Sunday morning she disappeared.

Every detail was perfect, the pink ruffled dress, the navy-blue blazer, even the gold locket on a chain around the neck.

Robin stared down at the figure, mesmerized by its lifelike quality.

Just as the little white barge started floating under the bridge, the figure's eyes opened and gazed up at her. They were big and bright and brown. A faint but unmistakable smile appeared on the childish lips.

Robin screamed.

Her scream echoed and died away across the still, black lake.

She gripped tight to the bridge's elaborately scrolled railing and called once more.

"Help. Help!"

But no one appeared.

Not a sound could be heard except her own harsh breathing.

A violent streak of lightning split the sky and lit the entire landscape. Simultaneously came a cataclysmic crash of thunder.

When the sound and light died away, the little white barge had disappeared.

When she reached the parking lot at the end of the bridge, the police car with its revolving lights was nowhere to be seen.

* * *

The wind began to blow and the rain poured in torrents.

Feeling sure by then that she would never leave the park alive, Robin staggered through the storm, trying desperately to find some exit—even a signpost indicating a way out of the vast black rainswept wilderness of paths and shrubbery and meadows and trees in which she found herself.

Every part of it was foreign territory.

In the heart of New York City, it was as though she had been transported to the abode of some malevolent genie, set down in a maze of mysterious disconnected landscapes, which might be perfectly charming in daylight, but at night seemed a Minotaur's labyrinth of unearthly terrors and surprises.

Every detail of the park was not only new to her, but imbued with the special horror she had felt for the place as a child. And her fear confused her, so that she chose wrong turns and performed panicky double-backs. Besides, as she staggered on past shadowy playgrounds and a huge weird statue of Alice in Wonderland sitting cross-legged on a mushroom, and a clock where a drummer-bear began to dance to a chiming little tune, she was assailed by grotesque phantoms melting out of the rainy night, as though they had been sent to confuse her further and head her off from any avenue of escape.

She was crossing a lonely ampitheater against the driving rain when "Madame Gautier" loomed out of the downpour in her starched white nurse's cap with her blue cape billowing. Smiling and grimacing, she hurried by, pointing to her torn throat, which was covered with blood and split open like a fish's mouth.

She looked shockingly real. Perhaps she was a dummy made of papier-mâché, or an actress dressed in a costume and made up to look ghastly, but in that lonely open-air theater with its white music shell and silent, stacked-up seats, she frightened Robin so that her heart felt ready to burst.

And in her confusion she took another wrong turn that

led her back to a melancholy plaza, like an antique palace courtyard with a rain-spattered cement pond and huge cement bowl
set in its middle.

Turning round to retrace her footsteps, she came face to
face with another fearful apparition—the old woman who had
risen from her bench like a snake and frightened Marya into
bolting that Sunday years ago. With her long black veil and her
straggling gray hair, she was even more evil-looking than Robin
remembered, as she crooked a bony finger and stuck her face so
close to Robin's that one could smell the musty odor of her
clothes, the foul stench of her rotted teeth.

The storm continued with unmitigated fury.

Robin stood in the midst of it, paralyzed and whimpering.

Her clothes were sopping. Her bare feet were icy. And
her hair hung in clammy strands about her shaking shoulders.

"God help me. Oh—somebody—please come—and
help me!"

It sounded like the wailing of a child or a lunatic. If
someone spied her now, they would call an ambulance and cart
her off to Bellevue for observation. For how could she ever explain
the diabolical crew that were bent on destroying her—mentally
or physically? No one would believe that people as devious as
the Kerenjis could exist—and no one would ever concede that
the illusions they had created to unbalance her reason were anything more than figments of her own imagination.

How clearly she saw now the full outlines of their plot-
ting. Having failed to complete their scam in Rouen, they had
sent Irène to New York as fresh bait, and Robin had fallen in
with their scheme completely. Skeptical or not about Irène's
protestations, she had given her the perfect opportunity to proclaim herself as Marya in the eyes of the world. From then on,
just as Jules Lefevre had said, all they had to do was kill her, or
failing that, proclaim her insane with grief and jealousy—so that
all the power and the wealth would fall into Irène's hands, or
rather the hands of Guy Kerenji, to do with as he pleased.

182 • LUCILLE FLETCHER

All her mother's talent and hard work, her father's genius and dedication to his art, would go into the coffers of a villainous actor and his murderous henchmen.

"Well . . . it isn't going to happen," she heard herself saying.

Somehow, in some way, she must pull herself together and escape from the park. She must survive—and destroy them.

Again, with her legs aching, her heart pounding, she began running.

Splashing through puddles, wading through wet grass, she saw the lights of Fifth Avenue coming closer and brighter. Then, out of the steady rain and the shadows, loomed a seemingly endless chain-link fence.

It blocked her path. It looked about twelve feet high. Construction of some kind was going on beyond it. She could see piles of dirt, heaps of broken concrete, and long stacks of pipes. And there was no way around it. She could only run along it, hoping to find an opening, but no opening could she see.

A policeman was approaching.

He was swinging a nightstick and carrying a flashlight. As he came toward her he stopped and turned it on. He flashed it in her face.

"What's the trouble, miss?"

She ran forward gratefully. "Oh, officer, I'm so glad to see you," she gasped—in the blazing glare of the powerful flash light. "I'm in trouble. A man is chasing me, trying to murder me."

"Is that so, lady?"

He came closer, She could see his face. Under the peaked cap, it was d'Egremont.

He reached out to grab her.

With a scream she ducked away and almost fell into a pile of dirt. Sobbing, she righted herself and veered off blindly from the chain-link fence. Behind her she could hear his feet pounding and the harsh rasping of his breath. And again it was a source of triumph, though not much comfort, to realize she could outrun him, as she had outrun the others.

* * *

Seeing him made her realize that the rest of the gang were probably pursuing her, but when the fence finally ended and the trees parted, she could see in the distance the crenellated towers of the old zoo arsenal she had thought was a king's castle as a child.

She remembered the arsenal as part of the big zoo plaza where she had stood at the age of eight looking around frantically for Marya. If she could reach it in safety, she knew she could find the steps to the winding path they had taken that Sunday morning—a path that led to the Fifth Avenue entrance, and all the life centered around the Plaza Hotel.

Making a final effort, she forced her weary legs forward, expecting at any moment to hear the gruff roar of a polar bear or the bark of a seal.

She stopped short, bewildered.

The zoo, as she had known it as a child, was gone.

It had become a wasteland of high board fences, piles of building materials, heaps of dirt. They must be making it over, but meanwhile it contained no animals, no cages, no seal pool, no restaurant, nothing but scattered cement foundations, deep holes, open spaces, board fences, and cement mixers.

She stood there, dazed, for a moment or two, caught off her guard, and suddenly became aware of shadows emerging from all sides of the construction site and heading silently toward her. She recognized the bulky shape of Voisin and a lanky shadow that had to be Sophie.

Instantly she ducked behind a high board fence, and suddenly encountered a man she did not recognize, lurking a few feet away with a chunk of concrete in his fist.

Drawing in her breath, she headed for a cement mixer halfway across an open space, only to see d'Egremont, still in his policeman's uniform, crouched behind it with his nightstick upraised.

Frozen with fear, she darted away, and as shadow after shadow emerged from the desolate ruins of the old zoo, she zigzagged desperately from one flimsy shelter to the next, crouching down and stumbling up, gasping with fear and lurching forward, until finally she reached the short flight of steps down which Marya had disappeared that October morning.

The path leading to Fifth Avenue appeared to be empty. Winding and narrow, with its old-fashioned streetlamps, deserted benches, and partially glimpsed view of the duck pond below, it looked like an escape hatch to heaven itself.

Trotting forward up its sloping incline, she could see the handsome shape of the Plaza, with lights blazing from its windows. She quickened her pace—but, rounding a curve, she spied a long black limousine waiting at the end of the path with its headlights on. She stopped short, and stepped quickly into a clump of bushes.

Shouts and footsteps sounded behind her. They were getting close, hot on the scent. Emerging from the bushes, she ran back to the steps, knowing that her only hope was to stay in the park and somehow outwit them. They had to be guarding all the south-side entrances. Everywhere she looked, she saw shadows advancing. None seemed to be on the path leading around the duck pond, and jumping down the last step, she headed down the narrow winding lane that circled the small weed-bordered body of water.

It was darker down there than on the lighted path above. It seemed far more sequestered and lonely and countrified. Woodsy shrubbery edged it on her left, and on her right, black water glimmered, spotted over with rain. Except for the neighboring skyscrapers, it was like a woodland lane. A swan glided by and she heard ducks quacking.

The shouts and footsteps sounded above her.

Blocking her way around the little lake were two sawhorses and beyond them construction materials and piles of dirt.

DANGER. KEEP OUT. NO PASSAGE BEYOND THIS POINT, said a sign posted next to a lantern.

She stood despairingly, looking back over her shoulder.

She heard someone wheezing and just above her, heading for the steps, was Voisin. He was waving to some invisible companion and surveying the darkness in all directions. In an instant, he might spy her, and she did not hesitate. Falling on her knees, she wriggled past the sawhorses and slid into the water. It felt pleasantly cool on her overheated body. The rain was still falling, spattering the surface with big drops. Stretching out, she lay down in the warmish shallow water next to the grassy bank and felt herself sinking deeper and deeper into mud, until only her shoulders and head were above the surface.

Hearing more shouts and the pounding of feet, she wriggled down even deeper, and gathering up handfuls of mud, began to smear her face, neck, and hair with muck. She laid her mud-covered face as far back as possible, keeping her nose and mouth barely above the water.

In this position she could breathe and see, but could hear nothing, for the water seeped into her ears unpleasantly.

She lay, trying not to move . . . trying to become one with the dark rustic landscape. A mosquito flitted about her eyes and she closed them, hoping he would go away. As she lay there like some half-submerged log, she wondered if snakes and rats lived along these banks—and if the water she was lying in was polluted.

But what did it matter so long as they did not find her, and she remained alive to expose their evil ways.

The minutes passed, and then the hours. She grew cold and began to shiver. Her right leg fell asleep and her hands began to tingle, but she dared not move or even raise her head.

Finally, after what seemed an eternity, she opened her eyes and saw that the rain had stopped and the clouds were parting on a beautiful moon.

Still she lay, until the stars began to pale into morning. When she dared rise from the water and crawl out of the slippery ooze, the path above her was empty, and the black limousine was gone.

20

BAREFOOT AND DRIPPING, with her clothes like wet rags, Robin trailed home, and nobody stopped her. In fact the few people she passed seemed to take her appearance for granted, so full of the poor and homeless, the street people and the merely eccentric, is the city of New York.

Arriving in the lobby she found a crowd of milling reporters. Marianne was in a state of panic. At nine-fifteen the previous evening, after her brief appearance on television Robin's mother had died, and already the news services had bulletins out and were clamoring for more.

"Don't tell them anything," Robin said. "I'll make a statement later." She headed for her apartment, then stood weeping under a hot shower. Marianne brought coffee. She had another catastrophe to report. Suzanne had been mugged the previous night and was in the hospital with a broken arm and bruises. "It was at the hospital," Marianne said. "Around seven-thirty, before you arrived. She left your mother's room for a few minutes to go down to the cafeteria for some orange juice your mother wanted, and someone came up behind her and pushed her down the stairs. It was a good while before anybody found her."

"Horrible," said Robin. It was obvious that Suzanne had also been a victim of the Terrible Kerenjis. They had had to get rid of her, so they could replace her with the bleached-blond nurse, one of their accomplices.

Robin tried to sleep but her nerves would not let her. For the next two days she moved in a trance, grieving for her mother and yet seeing her radiant face looking blissfully at Irène—or reliving her own wild rainy flight through the park and the long hours she had spent lying submerged in the pond.

As circumspectly as possible, she made a statement to the newspaper people, denying that her sister had been found. "Someone who looked like her," she said, "tried to convince my mother on her deathbed that she was actually her missing child, but my mother was too ill to question her at length, and since then the girl has disappeared and presumably left the country."

Robin also gave orders to the lawyers to be prepared for any suit Irène might institute. She gave them the paper Irène had signed, and wrote a long report on all the things the inspector had told her. However, these precautions seemed to prove unnecessary—for after that scene at her mother's bedside, Irène was seen no more—neither in her furnished room nor at the Peter Pan statue.

Voisin, d'Egremont, and Sophie had also disappeared.

On the third day Andy called, and it was like the return of sunlight.

He was in Yosemite, on the outskirts of a campground near the Merced River. His voice sounded deeply concerned and distraught. "I just read about your mother in a three-day-old newspaper," he said. "And I'm sorry for you, Robin dear. Are you OK?"

She said not very, and then told him the whole story of that evening at the hospital, and the gang's attempt to kill her after her mother had "recognized" Irène.

"It was all my fault entirely," she said. "But I wanted to make my mother happy, and Irène had almost convinced me she was sincere."

"I'm sorry I wasn't around to stop you—and protect you from those bastards," he said. "But what I don't understand is why they felt they had to kill you. Wasn't it enough just for your mother to declare she was really her missing daughter?"

"No," Robin said. "Because I'd made it very plain that I didn't believe she was . . . and if I didn't, then she couldn't possibly share Mother's inheritance with me."

"But—did she need your opinion? Couldn't she have insisted you were prejudiced and jealous?" he asked. "Brought a lawsuit, demanding you recognize her rights?"

"Perhaps . . . but she knew darned well I'd have fought it. So—" Robin said wearily, "it was easier to kill me before I had a chance to get home and talk to our family lawyer . . . or the police . . . or anyone. With me gone, then Irène and the gang would get the whole inheritance—and no questions would be asked."

"God, darling!" he breathed over long-distance. "I can't believe those sons of bitches! But listen—I've asked for some time off and I hope to be east by the end of this week."

"Oh Andy, how wonderful."

"I've got some cleaning up at the office to do, but I'd like to be there for your mother's funeral. When is it to be?"

"She's already been cremated," Robin said. "That's what she wanted, And I'm taking her ashes to England to be buried beside my father."

He was silent. "Beautiful," he murmured. "But you shouldn't be alone. Would you like me to go with you?"

"I would love it."

She began to cry.

A week later they flew to London with her mother's ashes in an alabaster urn. Andy fended off the press so that none of the English newspapers knew they were there, and they were able to rent a car and drive to Surrey in peace.

She showed him the beautiful mansion her father had left her, which she was renting to an American computer manufacturer. Then they walked to the country churchyard, where the vicar met them and conducted a short service as her mother's ashes were interred in her father's grave.

Robin laid two bouquets of violets on the marble monument she had erected to her father's memory and would soon have engraved with her mother's name as well, for she had always believed they had loved each other above all others, and had been driven apart only because of their own pride and ambition. Tears filled her eyes as she thought of her mother's beauty and talent and ultimate loneliness, and remembered the time when she had last seen her father after a concert he had conducted at Lincoln Center, gray-haired and stooped, signing autographs for crowds of people and later asking her bitterly why her mother hadn't seen fit to come.

A light breeze blew and the grass in the graveyard rustled. A part of her life had ended, a turbulent life of sorrow and excitement, hope and despair, all overshadowed by the loss of Marya. What would happen now, she wondered, and would she ever be free to live her life in her own fashion—without fanfare or drama, perhaps in the most ordinary way—but at least in a manner that was altogether hers?

Arm in arm she and Andy walked slowly toward the car.

"Do you remember when I told you I wanted to save your life?" he asked.

"Yes . . ."

"Is it too soon to ask if you're ready to have me try?"

"Oh Andy . . ." She stopped walking and laid her head on his shoulder. She pressed her cheek against his brown tweed jacket. It felt rough and warm and wonderfully comforting in the chilly English air.

"Will you marry me, Robin?"

"Of course, darling."

She felt as though a door were opening—on a room with a fire and children at her feet.

The wedding would be simple. They agreed that under the circumstances it should be a quiet ceremony, without frills or conventional formalities. "We can drive into the country or pick some little church in New York," he said. "Whichever appeals to you." But she said she would rather have it on the terrace of the penthouse.

"It's so lovely right now with most of the flowers still in bloom," she said. "And there's plenty of room to have the reception outdoors. Maybe we could ask your Great-Aunt Violet and a couple of my friends, and your friends and some of mother's . . ."

He was frowning.

"I'm afraid poor Aunt Violet's too old to travel," he said, "and if we have her or a couple of your friends and mine we'll have to have them all—and that gets to be a hassle. No—look . . ." He put his arms around her as they stood in Penn Station (for he was resigning from the park service for good the following day). "Why don't we just have ourselves, and an old judge I know from law school will come over from Staten Island to perform the ceremony. Then let's close up the apartment, jump into the car, and drive up to New Hampshire to some mountain lake. We could even drive over the border into Canada . . ."

"It sounds fine, Andy," she said—although she had already visualized banks of white flowers, a string trio playing the "Siegfried Idyll," oceans of champagne, and a honeymoon in Hawaii.

"I'll make all the arrangements," he was saying, "so you just relax, and order us a cake, and buy that pretty lavender dress we looked at yesterday. I thought it was terrific."

"OK," she said, smiling. "I'd rather wear white, but if you like it, I'll get it."

"I love it," he said.

His train was being called and off he went, carrying his suitcase down the steps to the platform. And she watched his blond head disappear, yearning for him and wondering how she would ever get through the next four days without him.

Marianne had asked for time off to visit her daughter, Rose was on vacation, and Suzanne in Switzerland, so Robin cleaned all the silver, and scrubbed, waxed, and polished the big seven-room penthouse until everything shone. All the next day she worked on the terrace, washing the glass doors that led from the rooms and cleaning the wrought-iron furniture. The leaves were swept up and the flower beds weeded. She even cleaned the mildew off the pretty Italian statuary her mother had bought in the first flush of her marriage to the Hollywood plastic surgeon whom she'd divorced after one bored year.

On a warm sunny afternoon a day before the wedding, Robin sat hemming the lavender dress she would wear to the ceremony the following afternoon.

A helicopter flew overhead and boats passed on the river. Seldom had she felt so peaceful, so contented. The phone rang and she hoped it would be Andy, calling to tell her when he was arriving in New York. He'd been calling three or four times a day since he'd been in Washington.

It was Jules Lefevre.

"*Bonjour, mademoiselle.* How are you?" His voice, as usual, was full of concern. She had not heard from him since the death of her mother and her harrowing ordeal in Central Park. "I hope by now you are feeling much better."

"Oh very much, monsieur, I'm being married tomorrow."

"Married?"

"*Oui.* At five o'clock," she said.

He did not speak for a second or two. Then he said, "*Eh bien* . . . congratulations. And who is the lucky man?"

"His name is Luke Andrew Forrester."

"Luke—Andrew—Forrester," he said slowly. "That's a good name. Is he in the theater?"

"Oh no. He's a lawyer—with the National Park Service."

"*Vraiment?* And what is that, *pardon?*"

"The National Park Service? It looks after our country's parks. Some of them are huge—"

"Oh yes. But of course—the Yosemite . . . the Grand Canyon . . ."

"*Oui.* And many others."

"How lucky for him. So interesting a life." He cleared his throat. "I have some news for you, mademoiselle. Did you ever at one time have a certain nursemaid named Katya Mirs?"

"Katya Mirs?" Robin frowned, and her puzzlement was no doubt reflected on the other end, for Lefevre said quickly,

"She's Polish—with very wide cheekbones, blond hair— blue eyes . . ."

"Oh yes," Robin interrupted. "Katty. She worked for us when I was seven—when my mother was in Hollywood, but not for long. She made too many passes at my father."

Lefevre chuckled.

"It wasn't funny. Mother fired her. And didn't speak to my father for at least a week."

"*Pardon, mademoiselle.* I didn't mean to laugh. But she was with you, then, before the kidnapping?"

"Yes . . . Mother had made the picture earlier that year . . . but what is this about, inspector?"

"Please call me Jules. It's just that she was picked up a week ago in Paris—for shoplifting. They learned that she had recently been involved with the Kerenjis. In fact—" he paused, "she was their researcher!"

"Oh no. Oh—Jules . . . !"

"So that might easily explain," he said slowly and deliberately—"Irène's reference to that monkey . . . that Zoom . . . zoom . . ."

"*Zumgolly!*"

Robin's voice was exultant. She had never forgotten that moment at the hospital, or been able to explain that haunting name out of the past. But here it was, on the eve of her wedding—a gift that would forever put an end to any lingering doubt about Irène's evil intentions and connections to the Kerenjis.

"Oh thank you—thank you," she kept saying, as he listened silently on the other end.

When she stopped at last, he said in a grave tone, "I'm very glad for your sake, Robin—but please don't relax your vigilance too quickly. They are not yet captured, and Irène's where-abouts are still unknown."

"But they wouldn't have the nerve *now*, I'm sure, in-spector," she said.

"*Peut-être*," he replied. "But one never knows with them." He broke off, and then added in a voice that labored to sound casual and cheerful, "However, I'm relieved to think you will soon have a husband to protect you. My good wishes to you, mademoiselle, and I hope you will be very happy."

"Thank you, Jules."

But he had hung up.

Poor Jules. She knew very well that she would never hear from him again. He was so proud and his feelings ran so deep that it probably would be wrong to write to him or try to keep in touch after her marriage. And Andy undoubtedly would resent any contact. After tomorrow she would have no need to call upon Jules for anything.

The thought somehow filled her with melancholy.

Andy arrived the following morning, the epitome of health, vigor, and good humor. She had never seen him in better spirits. His eyes sparkled, his laugh was hearty, and he lifted her up off her feet and would have raised her high in the air if she hadn't protested amid shrieks and laughter that he'd ruin himself for their wedding night.

He loved the way the apartment looked and went around admiring her handiwork. "You're an artist, Robin. You're the *real* artist in your family." He had bought her two new tapes and soon the penthouse began to resound with Delius's "Walk to the Paradise Garden" conducted by her father (it brought tears to her eyes) and then to cheer her up, he put on a new rock number by a group called Raw Flesh. It set the walls to vibrating and the crystal chandeliers tinkling.

"Let's dance." He seized her hand, and like a teenager, pulled her out on the terrace, where they went dancing up and down the bricks and the flagstones past the flower beds and wisteria vine and the freshly washed cupids and nymphs on their pedestals—while the jets criss-crossed the cloudless sky above their heads in a frenzy of silver patterns.

At four it was time to dress. Judge Callahan was due at five. Everything was ready, the two bottles of Dom Pérignon, the Venetian flutes her mother had adored, the embroidered tablecloth and napkins from Madeira and the Meissen plates for the cake—except for the cake itself, which had not yet been delivered.

"I'll look out for it," said Andy. "Why don't you go in and shower?"

While she was in the shower, she heard the buzzer sound, and a few minutes later, Andy knocked on her door, and when she opened it, there he stood, with the prettiest little cake she had ever seen.

It was ornamented with roses and violets and on top were two beautiful white doves kissing each other.

"Isn't it gorgeous?"

"Terrific." He beamed. "Oh darling." He kissed her bare shoulder above the terry-cloth sarong. "Everything you do is in exquisite taste."

"I know." She kissed him back. "I picked you."

"Now, don't ruin the cake . . ."

He carried it away.

By four-thirty she was dressed, and he came to look her over as she stood in the middle of her bedroom in the lavender dress with lavender slippers to match. Her black hair, at his request, was coiled into a *chignon*, which she had ornamented with her mother's diamond pin.

His eyes shone as he turned her around slowly. "Beautiful." he whispered hoarsely. He touched her cheek as though it were made of glass. "But may I make one small suggestion?"

"Certainly. What is it?"

He had his hand behind his back. With the other, very gently, he removed the diamond pin from her hair. "It's too artificial, too elaborate," he said. "Try this instead—OK?" In his left hand he was holding a small silk orchid. Deftly he tucked it into her hair. "It's simpler but more elegant—and it matches the dress."

"But of course, Andy . . ."

She didn't like silk flowers. She preferred the diamond pin. But it was *his* wedding too. "I love flowers in women's hair," he said. "It makes them look so virginal . . ."

He was still getting dressed in the guest room when the judge arrived at ten minutes of five. He was a frail-looking old man with a hectic flush on his cheeks, dark nervous eyes, and a white thatch of hair. He carried a black robe over his arm, and was accompanied by two witnesses for the ceremony.

"Is there a bathroom somewhere, where I can put this on?" he asked, after stepping out of the private elevator.

"Certainly, sir."

She led him down the hall past her mother's darkened bedroom, noticing, as they headed onward toward her room at the far end, that her mother's door was ajar and a dim light was streaming through the crack.

"Here we are, sir."

Smiling, she clicked on the lights in her bedroom and bathroom.

"Thank you, my dear." He flashed his false teeth. "I'll be right with you."

As he closed the door of her bathroom, she walked quietly to her mother's room.

It had not been used since her mother's death. All the jewels and clothes were still in the bureaus and ample closets. In fact the door had been kept locked and the curtains at the glass doors drawn so that Robin in her loneliness would not have to see the big lace bed, the sumptuous Egyptian bathroom, and the old pine rocker standing shadowy in the dark.

But the door was ajar—and *someone* was in there . . . someone unknown. She had seen a flash of lavender . . . the outline of a woman's head.

Cautiously she approached the slightly open door. Dim light still illumined the room beyond. Gazing across the lace bedspread and the tumbled lace pillows, she stared toward the bathroom, where a full-length mirror that had often reflected her mother's svelte figure glimmered in the eerie glow of her mother's old dressing-table mirror, with its circle of electric bulbs, a few of which appeared to be lit.

In front of the old theatrical mirror a girl was standing with her back to Robin—a girl in lavender with a petal-like chiffon skirt, a girl with black hair done in a *chignon* in which a lavender silk orchid was tucked.

From her head to her feet in lavender slippers, she was the mirror image of Robin peering in at her.

In fact, for a second or two Robin thought she was seeing a reflection of herself.

She was gazing at her own image, dressed for a wedding. She was seeing her own face, with its wide-set gray eyes, its heavy black eyebrows, and high Slavic cheekbones reproduced in the mirror with terrifying realism.

A cold tide of fear rose in her body.

As she watched, hypnotized, from the bedroom doorway, the reflection turned her head and smiled at herself coyly. Then, tossing her head back, the girl studied her profile and, staring full-faced into the mirror once more, tucked in a stray lock of black hair exactly as Robin might have tucked in and smoothed her own sleek coiffure.

Robin's heart seemed to stop. Her whole being sickened as the girl in the mirror smirked and grimaced and mimicked Robin's typical mannerisms.

What did it mean? And what did it portend? A whole new dimension filled her mind, and her world reeled, and as she stood there, silent and motionless, she knew, without following any process of logic, that Death was smiling at her from that glaring circle of light bulbs.

Irène had returned to the penthouse . . .

And Andy had let her in.

He had matched the orchid with the orchid—since there was only one antique diamond pin . . .

Lightning revelations flashed through her mind—and they were far more terrifying than the horrors of Central Park.

Yet somehow she had the presence of mind to step soundlessly out of the half-open door, back into the hallway.

21

"ROBIN, the judge is here . . ."

Andy was calling from the terrace in a voice so softly Southern and mellifluous that for a second she had the illusion that the girl in the mirror had been a trick of the light, and all was as before, normal and familiar and good.

"Robin, where are you?"

She had loved him for so long. She had thrilled to be near him. It was next to impossible to believe he was an actor, mouthing lies in all those love scenes, and covering her body with kisses with only murder in his mind.

"Robin . . . ?"

Her knees shook and her palms were clammy as she tiptoed down the hall toward the private elevator. With a shaking finger she pressed the button.

There was no response from the starting mechanism.

Again she pressed the buzzer and listened for the click of the car door as the car started upward, and the whine of its windy ascent up the elevator shaft. Instead, she heard only footsteps striding into the living room and Andy's smooth voice.

"Where are you, darling?"

Smiling, he stood in the living-room doorway—gleamingly handsome in his gray trousers and black jacket. Ruffles graced his wrists and the collar of his white shirt, but gazing into his eyes, seeing the coldness behind the twinkle, she felt no admiration, only loathing—and utter panic.

"Oh, there you are!" he was saying. "Anything the matter?"

"N-no. Not a thing . . . dear."

"Come in and meet the judge . . ." He put out his hand and tried to take hers, but she stepped aside, forcing a feeble smile.

"I've already met him."

"Oh have you . . . .?" Easily he smiled. "Funny old guy, right? He's aged since I saw him last. And he seems a little bit confused. He's deaf, you know, and he's just informed me that he's forgotten his hearing aid."

"Oh dear," she said as, with arm around her, he led her through the living room toward the terrace. "Then he can't marry us."

"Of course he can." He laughed his easy laugh. "He knows the words by heart. And we can shout the responses."

She echoed his laugh in a metallic sort of way, then turned from the glass door leading to the terrace, where the judge was standing in his long black robe, flanked by the witnesses.

"I—I must get a match for the candles."

Bolting out of the living room, she started down the hall. At its far end was the kitchen and the service exit leading to the basement—twenty-five stories down.

She heard Andy's footsteps behind her.

"I've got a match right here."

He was so cool, so casual, so nonchalant in his behavior it was hard to believe he wasn't the old charming Andy. But then he had played the role long enough by this time to fall into it at a moment's notice almost mechanically.

Who was he? Which one of the Kerenjis had been assigned to seduce her—providing an ace in the hole in case the caper in Rouen built around Irène didn't work out?

"What's wrong with you, darling?" He hooked his arm through hers, guiding her back to the living room. "Nervous? Got the bridal jitters?"

"Oh . . . scarcely," she answered hoarsely, realizing how poor an actress she was, a disgrace to her mother, who had been the essence of professional sangfroid.

Her mother had been able to act when her heart was broken. She could play a scene on the eve of a divorce, and still act in films when her child was missing. But Robin wondered how much of a trouper her mother might have been if confronted with the situation Robin found herself in—her beloved bridegroom a monster who had courted her only to destroy her—and his assistant in lavender, waiting to help with the murder and impersonate her after she was dead—so that no one would know Robin Chodoff was no more, since someone exactly like her had taken her place.

Robin knew that her mind was reeling.

Swaying, she stood beside the refreshment table in the living room, watching Andy strike the match and hand it to her with a smile, whereupon she tried to apply it to the tall white candle with a trembling hand.

"You *are* jittery, darling. Would you like an aspirin?"

"No thanks. I—I'm OK . . ."

There were six white candles in the elaborate silver candelabra, which three days ago, humming to herself, she had cleaned with an old toothbrush and polished to a gleaming brilliance worthy of one of her mother's old-time Hollywood butlers.

"Now the next one, darling."

He stood watching her every move, as one by one the candles flared into flame. He followed her, as, lifting the candelabra unsteadily, she carried the six flickering lights out to the terrace and set them on the glass topped table, in front of which the ceremony would take place.

On this late-August afternoon the air was still and the flames stood straight up with not a breeze to send them guttering.

They were dripless candles. She had bought them yesterday in a drugstore next to the bakery where she had ordered the wedding cake.

Where could she go? What could she do? Could she hide in a broom closet or a bathroom with the latch on? The service stairs were too far away and too steep and endless to attempt. Obviously he had jammed the mechanism on the private elevator—so how could she escape him on this pinnacle in the sky once he knew she was afraid—once he sensed that she had seen the girl?

"OK, sweetheart. Ready?" Shooting his white ruffles and smiling his fake smile, he put his arm around her again. "Judge Callahan," he called, "we're ready for the ceremony."

"Right away. Yes indeed." The old man hobbled toward them in his long black robe after Andy had called him a couple more times. His eyes darted everywhere under the unruly white hair. "Fine. Fine . . . Will you take your places, please?"

He stood on the terrace behind the glass table with the candlelight outlining the skeletal contours of his cheeks and false teeth. He motioned them to come forward. She felt Andy grip her hand with fingers of steel.

Sagging, she stood beside him with her head drooping, her eyes starting from her head.

She was seeing her own future . . . in a plastic trash bag dumped on Ward's Island, while here at the penthouse, her black-haired understudy, her perfect replica, palmed herself off as the new Mrs. Andrew Forrester, down to the last gesture, the last stock phrase, the last gullible smile.

"Dearly beloved, we are gathered together . . ." The judge sounded a little mixed up. He had launched into the religious ceremony. But what did it matter? This was not a real wedding, but only a charade performed for her benefit—so she would sign her name on the marriage certificate, giving Andy his conjugal share of her fortune.

And after that—into the trash bag.

A wave of nausea surged through her. She thought of

Madame Gautier, sprawled on the bloody linoleum with her eyes fixed and staring into space.

"Do you, Luke Andrew Forrester, take this woman, Robin Judith Chodoff, to be your lawful wedded wife?"

The judge was blinking with twitching dark eyes beneath his bushy white eyebrows. And Andy was looking solemn and very awed, like a real bridegroom being married to a woman he loved.

"I do."

His grip tightened on her chilly fingers.

"And do you, Robin Judith Chodoff, take this man, Luke Andrew Forrester, to be your lawful wedded husband?"

Was the judge a real judge, or just another member of the Kerenji troupe? Some old broken-down bit player, an "extra" like those old souls in the dining room of the Pension Bertrand, who had munched their rolls and gazed curiously at "Irène" in return, perhaps, for a couple of francs apiece?

"Robin—?"

Andy was looking at her as she stood daydreaming, his blue eyes narrowed into slits.

She forced a smile.

"I—do . . ." she choked.

The candles flickered, casting long thin shadows over the statuary and the pots of impatiens and aguretum. And overhead, in the darkening sky, a jet stream started upward, like a tiny star with a long silvery tail . . . a newborn comet.

"And now, by the authority vested in me," the judge was intoning, "by the state of New York and Almighty God, I pronounce you man and wife . . ."

Andy was slipping the gold ring, the one he had said was his mother's, on her finger . . . and drawing her to him, and kissing her on the lips. And it was time for the Mendelssohn, the burst of trumpets in a fanfare of triumph—and the crash of the full organ as the bride and groom marched out.

But the only sound was the roar of the traffic hurling along the East River Drive and the honking of rush-hour taxi horns, the shrill sounds of doormen's whistles in the streets far far below.

"You may kiss the bride, Andrew," said the judge, who had evidently not seen the previous kiss. He giggled.

"Gladly. *Dear* Robin . . ." He turned to her again with his burning blue eyes, and again she felt his kiss, warm and wet upon her mouth.

She stood rigidly, fearing him and loathing him, and yet aware of his enormous charisma, the pressure of his powerful masculine body, the clasp of his arms that she had so loved. Oh, what a stupid fool she had been to fall in love with him so easily, and believe every word he'd said . . . and yet half her trouble had been her deep and bottomless need for love and affection, her lonely buffeted childhood with two egotistical temperamental parents, and her feeling of guilt that *she* had been responsible for the loss of Marya . . . and could never never atone for that.

"All right, sweetheart, shall we sign our names? And then the judge has got to go . . ." He was breaking away, striding into the living room. "Come along, darling." He snapped his fingers. "Then it's off to New Hampshire." He swept past the champagne bottles and the wedding cake on its lace doily. "We should leave before dark."

"You won't stay for some champagne, Judge Callahan?"

"I'm afraid not, my dear. My wife is expecting me."

Andy led the way to the library, and she dragged along behind him and the old man, looking about for weapons, still pondering escape routes. A clothes closet with an inside latch? A bathroom with a door she could lock? None of them had windows, and they could trap her in there, barricade her and leave her, until she suffocated or starved to death. The more she thought about possible places to hide, the more hopeless she felt. Once the judge was gone, they would strike without mercy, and the only way she could leave this rooftop prison was to hurl herself over the terrace wall to the street twenty-five stories below.

"Here we are, honey. Here's the certificate."

In the library, under the brass lamp, he had spread out the official-looking paper and was holding up a gold fountain pen, her mother's.

"In a minute . . ."

As she went past the champagne bottles, she picked up the corkscrew and hid it in the folds of her skirt.

"What's the problem, darling? You seem very tense."

"Not a bit, Andy." She smiled. "I'm happy, that's all . . . it's making me sort of drunk."

"Well, good. But don't get too drunk, so you can't sign your name." He pointed to the place, and she could see the golden fuzz on the back of his fingers shining in the light. "Right here."

She sat down in the red leather chair. "No, you first, Andy." She looked up at him and smiled. "Men go first."

"Not in this day and age, baby." What nonsense they were talking. Soon the slaughter would begin. Once the judge left—though maybe if Andy was impatient, they would let him stay and help with her disposal. Would they cut her into little pieces—and flush them down the toilet? Or carry her body *in toto* in the trash bag down the service stairs, stuff it into the trunk of the rented car she had hired for their trip to New Hampshire, and head for the garbage dumps of Wards Island instead?

How would they kill her—with a knife? Like Madame Gautier? Or would Andy strangle her with his strong hairy hands? Or maybe the girl in lavender would hit her on the head with the silver candelabra.

Her eyes fell upon the candles. Out there on the terrace they were still burning—tall and straight. So white. So pure. Like six nuns in snowy habits, standing silently at prayer.

"Let's go, honey." His voice had taken on a sharper edge. He gave her shoulders a shove. "Try to concentrate. Judge Callahan's in a *hurry*."

"All right, Andy. I'm sorry . . ."

His leg was next to her, close to the seat of her chair.

She pushed in the corkscrew hard—into his thigh. And when he yelled, she darted past him out to the terrace, straight to the candelabra.

She lifted it and brandished it at him as he came limping toward her with his jaw set and his eyes ablaze. As he approached her, she touched the candles to the old dry satin draperies.

They hadn't been cleaned since her mother's illness. They had never been fireproofed. Their lining had rotted. And now, as the candle flames touched them, they began to sizzle and blacken.

"Give me that thing. Lay off. Are you crazy?"

He was shouting at her, but she only laughed and waved the candelabra more wildly to and fro. Smoke began to drift from the places she had set on fire, and better to burn the whole penthouse down, burn the antiques and the rugs and all the clothes, than die by slow inches at the point of a blade. And maybe somebody would notice the smoke rising from the roof and call the fire department, who would certainly be able to get up the service stairs, or turn the electricity back on in the private elevator.

The flames were tiny red tongues, licking at the curtains, making rents in the pale blue satin. Some had reached the floor and were dancing merrily along the priceless Aubusson rug. The judge had disappeared. So had Andy, but then she saw them both coming back with buckets of water, followed by the girl in lavender, her spitting image. She was also carrying a pail of water, and it was slopping over onto her dress.

"Stop. Stop. Arrêtez," she cried shrilly.

The voice was Irène's—unmistakably. Irène!—though she no longer looked anything like Marya. Andy began throwing water at the draperies. Then he disappeared again, and she saw him emerging from the glass doors of her mother's room and crossing the shadowy terrace toward her. His movements were stealthy. He was carrying a knife.

She dropped the candelabra and ran.

But the flames and Irène were blocking the entrance to the living room and all she could do was try to bolt across the terrace and circle around to one of the glass doors leading to her own room or the guest room. As he grabbed for her, she tore herself loose, but he was after her in a second, fast and fierce as a leopard, and the only place to run was around and around the terrace. Blindly she started off in her high-heeled lavender shoes, but her heel caught in between the bricks, and he was on her in a flash . . . catching her by her hair, and jerking her to her knees.

"Bitch," he panted. "Crazy dumb bitch." In that moment as she gazed up at him in stark terror, she saw him for the first time without his smiling mask—saw the pure evil in his face, the cruelty, the madness.

Then, just as though a bolt of lightning had struck him, his arm flew out, and the knife clattered on the bricks. As his grip relaxed, his body began to jerk violently, and rising to her feet, she saw him spin around, with his eyes rolled up and his arms flailing wildly. Suddenly, heavily, he fell forward on his face.

He lay still.

Blood began spreading across the back of his black coat, seeping out of his sleeves over the white ruffles.

"Guy!" cried a voice, and Irène ran out of the smoke-filled living room. Her black wig was awry, and her lavender dress soaked. "Guy!" she screamed, as she ran toward Robin, brandishing a carving knife. "You killed him . . ." But even as the hysterical words issued from her lips and she lunged forward as if to plunge the knife in Robin's breast, she froze, as though turned to stone, and sagged slowly to her knees.

"Guy . . . .?" Dazed, she looked around the dark terrace and then at the sprawled body lying next to the brick wall. "Guy . . ." Her wig had fallen off and her brown hair cascaded down her shoulders. "Don't leave me." Blood was running down her dress, soaking the petal-like draperies, but putting her hand to her bosom as though to staunch it, she began painfully dragging herself toward him, until she fell with her head across his knees.

And then for a few seconds she lifted her head and gazed around emptily. At last her head went down and she moved no more.

Only then did the gunman emerge from his hiding place. Grimly he led Robin back to the cowering old "judge" and the ruined remains of the wedding feast. The witnesses had long since disappeared in the confusion.

22

ON A DARK OCTOBER MORNING, with the wind blowing rain through the streets, Robin and Inspector Lefevre went to the morgue, where three years before she had gone with her mother to look at the drowned girl with the wrong kind of birthmark.

All the sad ghosts of the past filled her mind, as she and Jules approached the small grim building, but uppermost was a feeling of vast relief and thankfulness that the two demons who had pursued her since Rouen were gone forever.

Jules had saved her.

After one phone call to the National Park Service, he had arranged to be flown immediately to New York. Hoping to catch his quarry off guard, he hadn't called her, and he might have gotten there in time to stop the wedding with a couple of arrests, except for Guy Kerenji's sabotage of the private elevator. Racing up the service stairs three steps at a time, he arrived at the back door out of breath just as Kerenji emerged on the terrace with a knife. The back door was locked, and he had had to smash it open. By then Robin was down on her knees, and with one well-aimed shot he had killed Kerenji, and after that, shot Irène, as she was brandishing the knife. "I'd much rather have captured them," he said in his quiet fashion, "and perhaps solved their other crimes. But I couldn't risk your life, *chérie.*" He smiled gravely, then stared at the ground.

"Jules, you're wonderful."

"No. Just a policeman."

They entered the silent morgue.

Fortunately no reporters seemed to be about. There were only a couple of attendants present and the young pathologist who had examined the bodies. He led them to the room where "Andy Forrester," born Guy Kerenji, and "Irène," whose name and origins were still unknown, lay on two slabs under two canvas sheets.

Slowly the young doctor drew back the sheet to reveal the pale corpse lying on the steel gurney, and feeling terrible curiosity, yet revulsion, Robin gazed down at the real "Andy" without his charisma, his winning Southern ways.

He lay stark naked, except for a few bandages, a breech-cloth between his thighs, and a line of red stitches across his hairy chest from which Jules Lefevre's bullet had been removed.

Here was the lean perfect body she had adored . . . the broad muscular chest on which she had laid her head. He lay under the glaring overhead lights and he looked strangely shrunken, insignificant, and old, although still beautifully formed and fit as a professional athlete.

Her gaze reluctantly moved to the ashen face. The blue eyes were partly open—with a cold reptilian stare. The nose was pinched. A few teeth were missing in the gaping mouth. Nothing about him resembled dashing "Andy Forrester." In fact, he was nondescript—except for his superb body. Makeup and talent had created his charisma. As she searched for some echo of the real man she had known, she found not a trace of the other roles she had seen him play—from Raoul Guzman to the bleached-blond nurse she had confronted at the hospital.

It occurred to her that basically he had been nothing but his roles. A human puppet, without heart and soul, living only in a world of caricatures and impersonations. He had probably had no feelings of his own—but had only mimicked superbly the passions of other people.

She turned to the inspector.

"Who was Guy Kerenji? Do you know what he was like?"

Jules smiled. "Non. Few people did. All I know is he was born the son of a well-known Hungarian actor and a beautiful English mother who died young. His father starred in a couple of horror films back in the thirties . . ."

"So my mother was right?"

"Your mother?"

"The first time she saw him she said he reminded her of a foreign actor whose name she'd forgotten but he'd been in a horror film around 1930. That must have been his father."

"No doubt. How did he react?"

"Oh, shrugged it off. He said he didn't see many foreign films."

"It still must have been a shock. He must have hated your mother."

"He did—and so did she hate him, evidently—from that evening on. She seemed to have an aversion to him . . . though she never said why . . . and perhaps she didn't know why. She was very psychic."

Again she stared at the washed-out empty face—with its nondescript features and glazed lizard's eyes. They still had the power to frighten her, and she turned away, moving closer to Jules, as he went on talking about Guy Kerenji's life.

"From what we know, his family was quite respectable, and why he turned to crime has never been revealed. Perhaps it was due to his mother's death or some rivalry with his father, and then again, perhaps, like many criminals I have known, he simply enjoyed violence and hurting people as a way of life. He also loved money—and luxury, cars, travel, nightclubs, gambling—and women. I understand he was insatiable and known as a brutal lover, although there was one girl he seemed to have stuck with off and on, for several years. She bore a child by him."

"Irène?"

"*Mais oui.* She must have been very young when he seduced her . . . scarcely more than a child herself. No one knows what happened to it either, and it's probably dead by now."

They walked over to the other sheeted corpse.

Robin noticed how gently the young doctor drew back the sheet, as though he hated to disturb the woman beneath it. When she saw "Irène," she gasped. She had expected to see a much older woman with a coarser face, perhaps raddled with the tiny scars of plastic surgery.

The girl lying on the slab was fresh-faced and beautiful—as Irène had been beautiful in every guise. Her brown-gold hair fell in luscious waves and her pretty upturned nose and delicately molded lips and chin were just as they had been when she impersonated Marya—in her long black coat and black cotton stockings—or her white flounced dress—or her blue angel costume that night in the hospital.

Death had not changed her essential features—or her exquisite beauty. She *still* looked like Marya, and Robin's youthful mother.

Robin swayed against the steel gurney, feeling the same strange sensations she had felt looking down at the small white coffin on the lake that night in the park. There were the pointed eyebrows—not painted, not dyed, but growing naturally; and there, hauntingly, was the poignant look of wistfulness, so sad, so real, that Robin almost expected the brown eyes to open and gaze at her with a pleading look—as Marya as a child had gazed when she wanted something.

She closed her eyes. She turned away, fighting belief with a dozen arguments.

It couldn't be Marya—soft gentle little Marya who had loved her, looked up to her, and held her hand so trustingly. How could the real Marya have betrayed and lied to her—and at the very end, tried to kill her with a carving knife?

"Are you OK? Miss Chodoff?"

"Y-yes," she faltered to the young doctor and Lefevre. "It's just the resemblance. It's amazing, remarkable."

"To your sister?" the doctor murmured.

Robin nodded. "I had thought they did it all with plastic surgery. With wigs and makeup. But this is really as she was?"

"Absolutely," the doctor answered. "She was a remarkably beautiful young woman."

Robin turned to Jules Lefevre. "Do they know anything at all about her?"

"I'm afraid not very much." He walked away from the corpse, although Robin lingered, still gazing at the exquisite face. "Her nationality is unknown. So is her real name, and her exact age. We know that Kerenji picked her up somewhere in Italy when she was very young."

"But she wasn't Italian?" Robin asked, feeling a strange pang in the pit of her stomach.

"We don't think so. Someone told me she'd been stolen by Gypsies from a wealthy family, but that's never been confirmed by any reliable source. And another rumor has it that she was traded by these same Gypsies to a Czechoslovakian circus, a very small one, who trained her as an equestrienne or as part of an acrobatic troupe. But again, all these stories are vague and merely hearsay. I've even heard that she was used by the Gypsies to sell cigarettes and trinkets along the road or in their encampments."

"But the Gypsies did steal her?"

"Who knows, Robin?" He shrugged. "Beautiful children are valuable assets to Gypsy tribes in Europe. And some of them belong in the tribe so it's hard to tell." Averting his face from her intense gaze he added, "In any case, in the course of his travels, Kerenji spotted her and added her to his gang, either for her talent or her looks, quite possibly for them both."

Robin took a deep breath. "How old was she when he found her?"

"We're not sure, but we think about ten or eleven."

"Ten or eleven . . . !"

He gazed at her sadly. "In the world she probably lived in, children grow up fast."

He turned back to the body. He gazed at it for a long somber moment. "Children are so very helpless," he said softly, "so out of control of their fate."

Moving closer to the still form, he turned to Robin. "And yet one can't really look at her and think she was too badly treated, had a hard time of it. If she had been, it would have left its mark."

"Do you think Kerenji loved her?"

Jules shrugged. "*C'est possible*, if such a man were capable of love for another person." Again he studied the pale motionless face. "In my opinion, though, it's obvious that *she* loved *him* very much. Any part he asked her to play, she did to the best of her ability, any lies she had to tell, any cruelty she had to wreak was OK with her, so long as he wished it. Obviously she never questioned the purpose of her work. She lived only to please him."

"Oh!" Robin cried. "That was so much like my sister!" With tears in her eyes, but struggling to control herself, she added, "She never questioned, she just accepted. She wanted only to please people . . . to be loved . . ."

Her voice broke, and he stood looking at her with pity in his eyes. At last she brought herself to ask, "Do you—do you think she *could* have been Marya, or was it just coincidence that she looked so much like her?"

He was silent a long moment. Then he said very gently, "Perhaps he noticed a resemblance to your mother, and built his scam around it." His beautiful gray eyes rested on her a long moment. Then, touching her shoulder lightly, he said, "I think, *chérie*, you should think of her that way—as entirely his creation; otherwise your grief and suffering might never have an end."

"*C'est vrai*," she murmured and moved away as the doctor drew the sheet carefully over the face of the corpse.

But while the inspector was talking in another room, she

tiptoed back to the two steel gurneys and gingerly pulled back the canvas sheet from the face of the dead woman.

For several minutes she stood gazing in agony at the pretty, motionless, enigmatic face. Then, after a quick glance around, she placed her hand tentatively on the corpse's left cheek. It felt cold and clammy and strangely stiff, but overcoming her revulsion, she slid her fingers under the masses of brown hair and felt for the birthmark Irène had shown her on the night of their "contract."

Feeling only smooth skin under the thick hair, which kept falling back over her hand, she pushed the hair aside ever more feverishly until the dark-red heart-shaped birthmark came into view behind the left ear.

With haunted eyes she stared at it, and then ran her fingers over and over it, feeling for scars, raised skin, or stitches, anything that would prove it had been created surgically. While she was fingering it, the doctor walked in.

Quickly, with flaming cheeks, she pulled her hand away. As he walked up to her, she stammered, "I—I was just trying to find out if—if her birthmark was done by surgery."

He shook his head. "No," he said. "It was real. She was born with it."

23

OF ALL the cruel blows Robin had suffered, the fate of Marya was the most painful.

To think that her sister had deceived her and helped victimize her as she had victimized other people and finally tried to murder her was shocking indeed. But even worse was the realization of the amoral, heartless person Marya had become under Guy Kerenji's tutelage. Like a brainwashed zombie, she had done his bidding. The beautiful, gentle child had been corrupted into a changeling. And this terrible destruction had begun with the kidnapping.

How could it have happened? Robin tried to visualize what probably had occurred. Just the shock, the terror and bewilderment of Marya's capture, her panic and hysteria at being separated from her home and family must have traumatized her gentle, sensitive nature so badly it was a wonder she hadn't gone completely insane.

Perhaps, as she had once said to Robin, she had suffered from brain fever. And this had wiped out almost every last memory of her life on Fifty-seventh Street. Except perhaps for a few subconscious images and phrases. Zumgolly and Benny the turtle might have been real, not supplied by any computer or treacherous baby-sitter.

Whatever had happened to her—horrible or otherwise—
she had had to adjust to an altogether different life . . . perhaps
to poverty and filthy surroundings, people who neglected her or
tried to exploit her. When Robin thought of all the lives her
sister might have lived through, she could almost forgive her for
clinging so desperately to someone like Guy Kerenji, who for all
his evil ways, had been a constant, a substitute father-figure, a
family she could belong to. For Marya must have desperately
craved a family, and in her overwhelming need for love, learned
to close her eyes to the grotesque people Guy Kerenji hired,
learned perhaps to love them with pathetic loyalty. The Terrible
Kerenjis became her aunts and uncles, and Guy her Svengali,
whose words and wishes she never questioned.

Poor Marya . . .

Poor confused, immature, untutored Marya, floundering
her way through a world of shadows. Oh how much better, Robin
thought, if she'd been killed right then and there in Central Park,
as she kept remembering with searing pain the innocent little
figure in its pink ruffled dress, blue blazer, and long brown hair
skipping merrily along in her new patent-leather pumps.

For a long time after Jules left for France, Robin could
think of nothing but the traumas she had lived through and the
cruel injustices of life. But by late November she began trying
to restore some equilibrium to her days. She sold the big lonely
penthouse with its melancholy memories, all the furniture,
the jewelry, the fur coats, and expensive knickknacks, and gave
most of the money to charity in memory of her mother and
father.

Suzanne went back to Switzerland, where the huge bonus
Robin gave her enabled her to buy a small chalet near her family.
Marianne and Rose also received generous checks and glowing
letters of reference for future employers. For Robin did not need
them. She had lived long enough surrounded by wealth, and
had the overwhelming desire to strip her life down to the barest

essentials—to live sparely and plainly in some small apartment in Manhattan, and if possible, find a purpose that would bring her peace and joy.

The words of the old blind woman in Normandy returned to her thoughts from time to time. "God will somehow work a miracle if you trust Him and have faith."

In January she enrolled in law school and began running back and forth from her apartment to her classes. She made some new friends and they persuaded her to run with them in Central Park. By then she had lost most of her aversion to the place, and had stopped looking for "Voisin" and "Sophie" along every path, or in the streets or on the buses.

Yet they were still at large. Jules kept calling her from overseas with reports of their supposed whereabouts. He warned her not to cultivate anybody new without checking with him. If anyone suspicious tried to approach her, she was to phone him immediately.

In late April he phoned to say that all three men, "Voisin" and "Sophie" and "d'Egremont," had been captured in Corsica outside a café, and were in custody in Paris. They would be tried at the Palais de Justice. Would she be willing to come to France and testify?

On the fifth of May, Robin flew to Paris, where she was soon introduced to the intricacies of French law. The Palais de Justice fascinated and awed her, with its beautiful antique architecture and splendid high, gilded gates. She was impressed by the huge paneled room where the trial took place and the pageantry of the trial—the red-robed president and prosecutor in their ermine collars and black silk hats, and the lawyers in their black robes trimmed with ermine tails.

Mostly she was thrilled to see the three vicious criminals who had all tried to kill her behind their barricade of glass, flanked by *gendarmes*.

Shaved and well groomed, dressed in neat blue suits, white shirts, and ties, Sophie and Voisin and d'Egremont looked almost respectable—but the list of their crimes and the grisly details of the cases in which they had participated as actors—or assassins—belied their soft, almost inaudible testimony and their bland air of innocence.

Jules Lefevre spoke for two hours, testifying for the prosecution, and he was wonderful, precise, well informed, and sure of his facts. And after being rehearsed by a young woman attorney who flew around in high heels and gold hoop earrings, with ermine tails fluttering, Robin didn't do too badly herself.

After it was over, and the three handcuffed prisoners had been led out to a prison van, Jules drove her to his home in Saint-Malo to meet his children and his mother.

"She's been dying to meet you. She's a great fan of your mother. She's seen all her pictures several times, and now every evening we look at them on the VCR."

Robin laughed and shook her head. "Jules, you've got to be a saint!"

She loved Saint-Malo. He took her walking on "Les Remparts," a huge thick black wall that encircled the city. It looked very old, but he said it had been rebuilt entirely after the bombings of World War II. "Even the color and texture of the old stone was reproduced."

Like an immense black boulevard in the sky it stretched before them. It was wide enough for an army to march on. One could look out over the Channel for miles. The wind tugged at her hair and blew it back and forth, and she thought what fun it would be to run along this lofty promenade, breathing the fresh air and seeing the boats come in and out. He took her arm and told her about the tides that sometimes rose to heights of fifty or sixty feet in winter, so high that they sent great cascades of spray up over the black walls, spilling over into the town below.

Most of the old parts of the city were clustered inside the great walls—tall narrow houses like crowded toys inside a box. After a while he stopped talking, and holding tight to her arm, finally stopped walking and faced her.

"Robin, I have something to ask you. Were you serious about adopting that boy at the pension?"

Her heart leaped.

"You mean Jean-Pierre? Have you found him?"

He nodded, looking grave.

"Is he all right? He isn't dead?"

"No, he isn't dead," he answered slowly. "But he's had a hard time of it. His parents abandoned him."

"Where? Who are they?"

"In Spain," he said. "That's where they all fled at first, after the murder. And there, a month later, they left him outside Algeciras to fend for himself. He's only seven, you know, and shy, and speaks no Spanish, so he practically starved."

"Oh—poor little fellow. What kind of parents would do such a thing?"

"But that's not the whole story," he said, and then stopped.

"What *is* the whole story? Is he sick? He's been abused?" she asked, feeling a lump begin to gather in her throat.

Jules shook his head.

"No . . . he's OK. He's recovered—somewhat." Again he paused. "It's just—his parentage."

"What about his parentage?"

"I didn't know until Sophie confessed who his mother and father were."

"Who were they?"

Jules looked at her somberly. "Can't you guess?" he asked softly.

"Guy?" she whispered. "Irène?"

He nodded, and she stood there, hearing the wild surf beating against the rocks. And then, not far away, she saw three little figures coming along the immense black promenade—two dark-haired little boys toddling along on either side of a taller one with blond hair and blue eyes, who was leading them by the hand.

"Jean-Pierre!" cried Robin.

When he heard her voice, he stopped and smiled.

And maybe it was a trick of the light, but in the wistful shyness of that smile, she saw the ghost of four-year-old Marya gazing at her from the long-lost past.

"Oh Jean-Pierre!"

Weeping, she ran forward with arms outstretched.

Avon Books presents
your worst nightmares—

...haunted houses

ADDISON HOUSE   75587-4/$4.50 US/$5.95 Can
Clare McNally

THE ARCHITECTURE OF FEAR
                         70553-2/$3.95 US/$4.95 Can
edited by Kathryn Cramer & Peter D. Pautz

...unspeakable evil

HAUNTING WOMEN   89881-0/$3.95 US/$4.95 Can
edited by Alan Ryan

TROPICAL CHILLS   75500-9/$3.95 US/$4.95 Can
edited by Tim Sullivan

...blood lust

THE HUNGER   70441-2/$4.50 US/$5.95 Can
THE WOLFEN   70440-4/$4.50 US/$5.95 Can
Whitley Strieber